Critical Acclaim
for Bruce Jay Friedman's *The Lonely Guy:*

"Sparkling . . . sly . . . engrossing . . . winsome and true. I can imagine no book that would be more appropriate reading, propped up against the Blue Plate Special in a cafeteria on Father's Day."
— Herbert Gold, *The New York Times Book Review*

"Will be around as long as there is humor in the American fiber. It is the funniest book of this year, or most any other. You don't close this book. You just start reading it again immediately. I loved every page—and laughed out loud on most of them."
—Dan Jenkins, author of *Semi-Tough* and *Dead Solid Perfect*

"A book to make you laugh out loud—and to make you see. On one level, this is sound entertainment. . . . On another level, Friedman appears to be getting at sober matters. . . . What makes this writing more than just the strutting of a stand-up comic is the pain whispering behind the gags."
— Peter LaSalle, *The New Republic*

"Three words that always make me laugh are Bruce Jay Friedman. I read *The Lonely Guy's Book of Life* and laughed. And laughed. And laughed. From the dedication on, he retains his ranking as one of the funniest writers in America."
— John Gregory Dunne, author of *True Confessions* and *The Studio*

Critical Acclaim
for Bruce Jay Friedman's *The Slightly Older Guy:*

"[A] funny little book . . . of what we might call urban folk knowledge, in that Friedman is imparting insights garnered from his own experiences. Whether slightly older guys should wear ponytails, having a slightly older wife as opposed to a younger wife, and being forced into retirement are among the subjects of Friedman's ruminations. . . . Entertaining . . . Funny stuff not just for Slightly Older Guys."
—*Booklist*

"A witty book on the midlife travails of the Slightly Older Guy (SOG). The SOG is concerned about enough bran, too many eggs, and when the medical profession will make up its mind about the prostate gland. This near-SOG reviewer is already uneasy with his new doctor, a mostly younger woman (MYW), whose attention is diverted annually to his prostate." —*Library Journal*

"Males over 50 will find the light touch of top humorist Friedman bringing smiles of recognition on page after page. The SOG will see himself in the man with wattles under his chin, a memory that is not totally reliable, and the recollection of that traumatic moment when the pretty girl he was ogling on the subway smiled and said, 'Would you like my seat?'" —*Publishers Weekly*

The
Lonely

Guy

and

The
Slightly

Older Guy

The Lonely
Guy
and
The Slightly
Older Guy

With a New Afterword by the Author,
"The Considerably Older Guy"

BRUCE JAY FRIEDMAN

Grove Press
New York

Published simultaneously in Canada
Printed in the United States of America

FIRST EDITION

Library of Congress Cataloging-in-Publication Data
Friedman, Bruce Jay, 1930–
[Lonely guy's book of life]
The lonely guy : featuring The lonely guy's book of life and The slightly older guy /
Bruce Jay Friedman ; with a new afterword by the author ;
illustrations by Drew Friedman.
p. cm
First work originally published: New York: McGraw-Hill, c1978; 2nd work
originally published: New York: Simon & Schuster, c1995.
ISBN 0-8021-3833-0
1. Single men—Humor.   2. Middle aged men—Humor.   3. Man-woman
relationships—Humor.   I. Friedman, Bruce Jay, 1930– Slightly older guy.
II. Title: Lonely guy's book of life.   III. Title: Slightly older guy.   IV. Title.
PS3556.R5 L6 2001
818'.5407—dc21
2001033481

Grove Press
841 Broadway
New York, NY 10003

01 02 03 04   10 9 8 7 6 5 4 3 2 1

For the Invincible Swiss Pikemen of Marignano—
Defeated by Francois I—1515

Contents

THE SLIGHTLY OLDER GUY

Introduction: Who (or What) Is a Slightly Older Guy?, 155

The
Lonely Guy

Illustrations by Victor Juhasz

To BJF
This one's for you, fella.

Introduction
Who Are the Lonely Guys?

Who are the Lonely Guys?
They tend to be a little bald and look as if they have been badly shaken up in a bus accident. Jules Feiffer obviously had "Lonely Guy" stamped on his forehead in the cradle. Buck Henry. Guys like that. But it gets tricky. Woody Allen is doubtful. We're not talking shy here. That's another book. The Shy Guy's book. Warren Beatty gets you mixed up because of all his dating. He may be a secret Lonely Guy. Why else would he have made *Shampoo*, which winds up with him on a hill, albeit a Beverly Hill, puzzling over the folly of the human condition? Jack Nicholson's too quirky.

Except for Truman, all presidents are Lonely Guys since they have to go off regularly and make decisions that affect the hearts and minds of all Americans for generations to come. They usually do that after lunch. One blooper, and that's it, for an entire generation to come. All of which makes for a tense Oval Office Lonely Guy. Was Nixon a Lonely Guy? Even at the crest of his powers, he ate a lot of Lonely Guy food. American cheese sandwiches and pale vanilla shakes. Until he started drinking those wines. Yet even his wines were Lonely Guy San Clemente wines.

Network heads are visionary Lonely Guys and so are the fellows in charge of FBI district branches. It's possible there are entire gay couples that are Lonely Guys. Women can be Lonely Guys, too. Female stand-up comics, for example. Also women who are sensitive but are trapped inside lovely faces

and bodies. Certain Wilhelmina models are in this pickle.
She's not going to be throwing any eggs in the pan at four
in the morning, but Jacqueline Onassis may be a Lonely Guy.
Kierkegaard was probably the first Modern Day Lonely Guy,
although he may have disqualified himself when he came
up with faith. (Lonely Guys know what the score is in this
department.) Howard Hughes went over the line when he
let those fingernails grow. Right fielders are Lonely Guys.
So are free safeties, doormen and large dogs. Horses are
Lonely Guys unless they are the spoiled favorites of girls
named Wendy in Darien. All of Canada may be a Lonely
Guy. "Boat People" thought they were Lonely Guys until
they got settled in suburban homes in Sacramento. Married
people are fond of saying that they are Lonely Guys, too. But
this is like marching in solidarity for Choctaw rights, when
you're not a Choctaw. No Polish directors are Lonely Guys
since any time they like they can just reach out and grab a
script girl and some caviar.

Lonely Guys lean against railings a lot and stare off in the
distance with bunched-up jaw muscles. They had a bad time
at summer camp and are afraid they are going to be sent back
there, even at age forty. From the street, they peer in at cocktail lounges, through the potted palms, and decide the place
is not for them. They take naps in the early evening and are
delighted to wake up and find it's too late to go anywhere.
A favorite activity of the Lonely Guy is to take a walk down
by the river. Lonely Guys start to fill out forms with great
enthusiasm, then quickly lose heart, right around the part
that asks for their mother's maiden name.

This book is written not in celebration of the Lonely Guy,
since obviously there is not much to celebrate. But it is designed to let him know that someone is aware he is out there.
And that he is not alone. There are millions like him, even
though he has only a small chance of meeting the attractive
ones. The Lonely Guy may decide that he doesn't *need* a book,
but this is entirely beside the point. If he is going to co-exist

with his fellow Americans, he has got to learn to accept gracefully things he doesn't want.

The book may be picked up and read at any old place; the chapters do not follow in any rigid sequence, and in that sense, the book is like the Lonely Guy's life, one phase of it relentlessly like the next. Care has been taken to address the specific problems of the Lonely Guy—such as what to do with little leftover pieces of soap. On occasion, the reader will be led to the door of wisdom, only to be asked to wait outside for a while. The perceptive Lonely Guy will see that this approach, too, is a deliberate one, designed to mirror the quality of the life that awaits him. Never mind that it would have been much more work to write a book that actually delivers the goods.

Does life itself deliver the goods for today's Lonely Guy?

This book, finally, is your companion, Lonely Guy, a loyal comrade in the battle against a world you never made—and one that often seems to wish you would go away.

Read around in it, clutch it to your thin chest, and do not leave it on someone's buffet table.

BJF
Penn Station, 1978

Part One

The Basics

Brief Bio of a Lonely Guy

- He married a woman because she smelled like gardenias. She also did a perfect imitation of Cyd Charisse.
- They chose the suburban town in which they wanted to live because it had an attractively rustic name.
- They named their child after a bit player in a late-night movie.
- He picked his divorce lawyer because the fellow had an office in Madison Square Garden where the Knicks, Rangers and all his favorite teams played.

The Lonely Guy's Apartment

At college, he was quite shy with women. His approach was to say "Hi there," tell the woman his name and then say: "Some day I would like to have an apartment overlooking New York City's East River." He could not recall one instance in which a woman responded to this technique.

A Lonely Guy's best friend is his apartment. Granted, there is no way for him to put his arms around it, chuck it under the chin and take it to a Mets game. But it is very often all he has to come home to. Under no circumstances should he have an apartment that he feels is out to get him. One that's a little superior. An Oscar Wilde of an apartment. No Junior Studio will ever throw its arms around the Lonely Guy and say: "It's gonna be all right, babe." But it should at least be on his team. Perhaps not a partner on life's highway, but somewhere in his corner.

If you are a brand-new Lonely Guy, the chances are you have just been thrown out and have wound up draped over the end of somebody's couch. Either that or you have booked a room in an apartment-hotel for older folks who have Missed Out on Life. There will be a restaurant in this kind of hotel where people take a long time deciding if they should have the sole. You don't want to become one of those fellows. As soon as you get movement back in your legs, try to get your own place.

Many Lonely Guys will settle for a grim little one-roomer in which all they have to do is lie there—everything being in snatching distance of the bed—contact lens wetting solution, Ritz crackers, toothpicks, Valium, cotton balls, etc. This is a mistake. No Lonely Guy can thrive in an apartment that comes to an abrupt ending the second he walks through the door. There is no reason why he should have to go to the zoo for a change of scenery. Or stand in the closet. The Lonely Guy in a one-roomer will soon find himself tapping out messages to the next-door neighbors or clutching at the window guards and shouting: "No prison bars can hold me." It's important to have that second room even if it's a little bit of a thing and you have to crawl into it.

The best way to smoke out an apartment is to check with your friends. Everyone will know someone who has seven months to go on a lease and wants to sublet. Someone who's had a series shot out from under him. But this may not be the best way to go. Living in an apartment with seven months remaining on the lease is like always waiting for the toast to come up. Try to get one with a decent amount of time remaining, eighteen months or two years, so you can at least feel it's worth it to get your Monterey Jazz Festival posters on the wall.

Rental agents can be useful, except that they tend only to handle apartments with wood-burning fireplaces. If you say you don't want one, you get marked down as an uncharming fellow who didn't go to acceptable schools. The tendency of the new Lonely Guy will be to grab the first place that looks better than a Borneo Death Cell, just so he can get off the street. He doesn't want to make a career of looking at vacant apartments which still have other people's old noodles in the sink. It will be worth your while to hold out, to contain your retching just a few days longer and ask yourself these questions about any apartment before you snap it up:

How Is It for Taking Naps? Lonely Guys take a tremendous number of naps. They are an important weapon in the fight to kill off weekends. Before renting an apartment, make sure it has good nap potential. You might even want to borrow the keys from the rental agent, lie down and test-nap it.

What Would It Be Like to Have Bronchitis In? Bronchitis, that scourge of the Lonely Guy. Call up any Lonely Guy you know and he's likely to be in the last stages of it. (Lonely Guys don't wash their vegetables.) But it's an excellent test: Is this the kind of place I'd want to have Bronchitis in or would I feel ridiculous?

What About Noise? Tomb-like silence is not always the ticket. It can be dangerous for a Lonely Guy to sit around listening to his own pulse. Some noises aren't bad. The sound of an eminent chest specialist with a persistent hacking cough can be amusing. But make sure there isn't a lady above you named *Haughty Felice* whose specialty is chaining up stockbrokers and hurling them into play dungeons.

"Get in there, Dwight, and start worshipping my stiletto heels."

Nothing is more unsettling than to hear a commodities expert rattling his handcuffs at four in the morning.

Do I Want This Apartment Waiting for Me When I Get Back from San Francisco? The Lonely Guy may often be sent to San Francisco to whip a sluggish branch office into shape. When he returns, there will never be anyone waiting at the terminal to hail his arrival. This is always a clutch situation. The well-traveled Lonely Guy deals with it by holding back his tears and impatiently shouldering his way through the crowd, pretending he's got to catch a connecting flight to Madrid. Still and all, if he gets out of the airport at one in the morning, and there isn't a wonderful apartment waiting for him, all warmed up and ready to go, that could be it, right there, ring-a-ding-ding, into the toilet for good.

Is It Overpriced? The Lonely Guy has been taught two things, ever since he was a little tiny Lonely Guy: (1) Never kneel down to inhale bus exhaust fumes. (2) Keep the rent down.

It's time to take another look at that second one. All terrific apartments are overpriced. The only ones with low rents are downwind of French restaurants that didn't get any stars at all in dining-out guides.

When it comes to rent, it's probably best to cut down on other things, like molar insurance, and pay through the nose, if that's what it takes to get a winner. On the other hand, don't pay so much rent that you have to live on *Milk Duds*. Or that you're always mad at your apartment. Remember, it's not the apartment's fault that it's expensive. There is nothing the apartment can do about it. Can it help it if it's great?

Is This Apartment Really Me? That's the Big One. Freud told his followers that when it came to making major decisions they should listen to their "deep currents." You might find an apartment that would be just right for the early struggling Gore Vidal. Or for Harry Reasoner right now. But does it have *your* name on it? Listen to your deep apartment currents on this one. Ferenczi, a disciple of Freud's, listened to his and admittedly committed suicide. But not before he'd enjoyed many happy months in a charming little duplex in Vienna.

In sum, you need a great apartment.

There will be times when it will be just You and Your Apartment against the World.

Get yourself a stand-up apartment.

Here are some more apartment insights:

One Great Feature

Before you sign the lease, make sure the apartment has at least one special feature—a natural brick wall, a sunken living room, smoked mirrors—so that when you are walking around aimlessly, you can stop suddenly and say: "Jesus, look at those smoked mirrors. And they're all mine, until the lease is up." That one terrific feature might even be a dignitary. Then you can go around saying: "I've got a little place in the same building as John Travolta's dermatologist."

Terrace Tips

The Lonely Guy with a decent income should try to get himself a terrace. The most important thing about a terrace is to make sure it's screwed on tight. A lot of them fall off and are never reported because people are too embarrassed, the way they used to be about rapes.

Along with the terrace, it's essential to get a Monkey Deflector. Many big-city buildings have South American diplomats living in them who keep monkeys that will swing in at you. Chileans are especially guilty of this practice. They will insist the monkeys are harmless—"Just give Toto a little yogurt"—but if you check with the doorman, you will find out they are biters.

Once you have a terrace, don't feel obliged to throw over your adult life to the care of potted flowers. Toss a few pieces of broken statuary out here and tell visitors: "I'm letting it go wild." This will impress women who have been raised in Sun Belt trailer courts.

The Joy of Lighting

Too much emphasis cannot be placed on the importance of good lighting. The Lonely Guy with an uncontrollable urge to bang his head on the refrigerator may be reacting to sallow, unattractive light. Lighting should be warm and cozy

and there should not be too much of it. An excess will remind
you that there isn't anyone wonderful in there with you. Too
little will have you tapping along the walls to get to the bathroom. A sure sign that the lighting is wrong is if you spend a
lot of time taking strolls through the building lobby.

Unfortunately, there is no way to tear off a piece of lighting you like and bring it down to the lighting fixture people.
There is no such thing as a swatch of lighting. One kind not
to duplicate is the harsh, gynecological type favored by el-
derly Japanese civil service officials who like to spy on their
sleeping nieces.

Lighting fixtures are tricky. Some will give off a cool and
elegant glow in the store, and then turn around and make your
place look like a massage parlor. The best way to get the lighting right is to experiment and be prepared to go through half
a dozen lamps to get the right one. It's that important. Some
of the finest light is given off by the new Luxo lamps. Unfortunately, they look like baby pterodactyls, and Lonely Guys
who've used them complain that their lamps are out to get
them. A great kind of lighting to have is the kind they have
at a bar you love in San Francisco. Shoot for that kind.

Views

The worst view you can have is a bridge, particularly a
Lost Horizon type that's obscured in fog at the far end. In no
time at all, the Lonely Guy will start thinking of it as a
metaphor for his life, stretching off into nowhere. Some other
things not to have as a view are prisons, consolidated laundries and medical institutes. The Pacific is not so hot either
unless you're into vastness. Interiors of courtyards are toler-
able, but will tend to make you feel you should be writing
a proletariat novel or at least in some way be clawing your
way to the top. The world's most unnerving view is when
you can see just a little bit of a movie marquee; the only way
to tell what's playing is to stretch all the way out the win-

dow while another Lonely Guy holds your ankles. The most relaxing view is the Botswana Embassy.

People Who Can Help You Decorate

The Last People Who Lived in the Apartment. When you move in, don't rearrange anything that was left behind. Chances are the previous tenant knew more about decorating than you do. He may even have been a tasteful Lonely Guy.

The Moving Men. Many have good decorating instincts, especially if they are out-of-work actors. A danger is that they will make your apartment look like an *Uncle Vanya* set. But if your own decorating instincts are shaky, leave things exactly where the moving men set them down.

Any Woman Who Worked on a Major Film. Invite one over, don't say a thing and have a normal evening. At some point, reflexively, she will move a sconce or something several inches and you will see a boring room explode with loveliness.

The Woman at the Department Store. Every department store has a handsome woman in her fifties who is assigned to help Lonely Guys. She will have a large bosom, generous haunches and will set you to thinking about Dickensian sex with your mother's best friend in front of a hearth. There is no need to seek her out. She will spot you at the door of the furniture department. (There is some evidence that she is in league with the divorce courts and that you may have been phoned in to her.) Work with this woman, though cautiously. No matter what your sensibility, she will see you as a craggy, seafaring type out of a late-night movie ("Dash my buttons if you aren't a handsome-looking sea-calf") and pick your furniture accordingly. Upon delivery, many of her choices will not fit through your front door. Why does she pick out furniture that's too big to fit in? No one knows. She earns no commissions on this massive stuff that has to go back to the store. It may have something to do with her ample haunches. Get her to try again by coming on smaller.

Fear of Decorators

Many people are terrified of decorators, afraid they're going to be given widely publicized Bad Taste Awards if they don't go along with every one of the decorator's recommendations. It's because of those "to the trade only" signs on all the good furniture stores. Just once, talk back to a decorator. The experience can be exhilarating.

> DECORATOR (a woman with orange hair): I've thought it over and you're getting Riviera Blinds for your living room.
> LONELY GUY: No, I'm not.
> DECORATOR (astonished): What?
> LONELY GUY: You heard me. I hate Riviera Blinds. And I'm beginning to hate you, too.
> DECORATOR: How about the track lighting I ordered?
> LONELY GUY: Hate it. Send it back.
> DECORATOR (after a pause): You're right on both counts. I'll get rid of the "verticals," too.
> LONELY GUY: The "verticals" stay. I've always had rather a fondness for "verticals."
> DECORATOR (with new respect): You're hard to work for . . . but *so* challenging.

A Word of Caution on Desks

The easiest thing to buy is a desk. Rough-hewn ones made of driftwood, rolltop desks, elegant French ones upon which the first acts of farces were written. The Lonely Guy must be careful not to buy a whole bunch of them; if he does, his apartment will soon look like the city room of a scrappy small-city daily.

Ashtrays

It's important to have a lot of ashtrays around and not just to accommodate smokers. When they cook, most Lonely Guys have nothing to bring the vegetables out in. Certain ashtrays can pass as a charming new kind of vegetable platter. The peas, for example, look just great in a big bright ashtray.

Bookshelves

Books give an apartment a scholarly pipe-smoking look. Many rock-oriented young women will assume you wrote all the books in your shelves—that you were once named Coleridge. Don't overdo it and turn your place into a library. The saddest book story is that of Lonely Gal Eleanor Barry (reprinted in its entirety from *The New York Times,* December 21, 1977).

A 70-year-old woman was pulled out from under a giant pile of books, newspapers and press clippings that had collapsed on her, but she died shortly after being rescued. The pile fell on Eleanor Barry as she lay in her bedroom, and according to police in Huntington Station, Long Island, the weight of the papers muffled her cries for help. She died Sunday.

The police said they had to use an axe to smash the door of the bedroom because the collapsed pile blocked their entry. They said that the house was filled with towers of books, newspapers, shopping bags and assorted papers.

The Ends of Things

It's important to put some focus on the ends of things as the Lonely Guy will be spending a great deal of time huddled over there in a corner. An investment in a bunch of good strong end tables, for example, will not be wasted. It's important, incidentally, to keep couches manageable in size and not have them stretching off in the distance. What's the

point of being the only fellow on a long freight train of a
couch! Other, juicier opportunities for loneliness and isolation will be coming your way. And stay away from Conversation Pits. The Lonely Guy who's rigged one up will quickly
see that he is the only one on hand to sound off on America's
lack of a clear-cut natural gas policy.

A Tricky Decision

Do you go with overhead mirrors? There is no question
that they are fiercely erotic, especially if you can talk an *au
pair* girl into slipping under one with you. But what about
those nights when you're just a poignant guy staring up at
his own hips! The makers of overhead mirrors are conservative and confidence-inspiring, many of them respected
Italian-Americans with no connections to the Gambino family. But they cannot absolutely guarantee that an overhead
won't come down in the middle of the night and turn you
into a whole bunch of Lonely Guys. For this reason, it might
be wise to pass.

Plants

Buy a lot of them. Scattered about, they will cover up the
fact that you don't have enough furniture and aren't knowledgeable about room dividers. A drawback is that each day
you will see little buds and shoots, life perpetuating itself
while yours may very well not be. Buy your plants on the
opposite side of town. They are always cheaper over there.
Refer to your plants as "Guys." Put your arm around one
and say: "This guy here is my avocado."

Room Freshener

Lonely Guy apartments tend to get a bit stale, so it's
important to load up on room fresheners. The way to apply

one is to hold it aloft, press the aerosol button and then streak through the rooms as though you are heralding the start of the new Olympics. Some of the fumes will flash back and freshen *you* up, along with the apartment. Many a woman who has admired a Lonely Guy's cologne is unwittingly in love with his room freshener.

A Sheet and Blanket Program

One kind of sheet to be wary of is the elastic bottom one that curls over the four corners of the bed and supposedly stays there. As soon as you buy them, they no longer fit. The biggest problem is that they tend to break loose in the night and snap you up in them.

Silky, satiny sheets feel good to the skin and will give you an inkling of what it's like to be Bob Guccione. But what you get is a combination of sleeping and ice-skating and there is always the danger of being squirted out of bed. Just buy colorful sheets you like.

The time to change sheets is when you can no longer ignore the Grielle and Zweiback crumbs in them.

Salesmen will tell you that East German llama blankets are the warmest in the world and are so tightly woven that the thinnest shaft of cold can't sneak in there and get at you. None of this is important. The only way to test a blanket is to hold it up to your cheek and see if it feels fluffy. (The sight of this is heartbreaking and will help you in picking up saleswomen.) Better to have ten fluffies than one llama that holds off chilly weather but has a hostile Cold War feel to it.

Shower Curtain Madness

The trick in getting a shower curtain is to find one that fits right. Shower curtains are either long, flowing things that look like gowns worn by transvestite members of the

Austro-Hungarian General Staff, or else they are shorties that will remind you of Midwestern insurance men whose pants don't come down far enough. Bob Dole fans.

There is the possibility that the Lonely Guy is incapable of buying any shower curtain at all. And that he will have to wait till Ms. Right comes along. If such is the case, and you plan to go without a shower curtain, the trick is to let the water hit your chest so that as much of it as possible bankshots back into the tub and doesn't rot your tiles. If enough of it gets out there, you will run the risk of plunging through the floor to the Lonely Guy below.

Silver Separators

Lonely Guys with mangled hands are usually assumed to be veterans of Iwo. This is not necessarily the case. Too often, it's a result of reaching into kitchen drawers to try to get knives and forks out. The way around this is to buy a silver separator that has little rows for utensils. On the other hand, many Lonely Guys would rather sever an occasional artery than stand around filing butter knives.*

Pictures You Are Not Sure Of

Lonely Guys have a tendency to accumulate paintings they are not quite sure of—gifts from dissident Haitians or suburban women who've suddenly left their families and moved into Soho lofts. The way to deal with such a painting is to prop it up on a dresser and put stuff in front of it—a clock, a Fundador bottle, a book about the fall of the once-proud

---

*Another way to deal with silverware is to slap it up in full view on a magnetic wallboard. However, the underweight Lonely Guy with a metal watchband runs the risk of being sucked right up on it, along with the knives.

Zulu nation—so that only some of the painting shows through. Make it look as if it's ready to be hung, but that you haven't gotten around to it. (You don't know where the nails are anyway.) That way, if someone admires it, she can push aside the obstructions and say, "Hey, whatcha got there, fella?" If she hates it, you're covered because you've put all that stuff in front of it, indicating you don't think it's so hot either.

The Right Air Conditioner

Get a strong, no-nonsense air conditioner that sends the cold air right up the middle at you. A Larry Csonka of an air conditioner. Don't get one in which the air wanders out in a vague and poetical manner so that you have to run around trying to trace it.

The Right TV Set

The most important thing about a TV set is to get it back against something and not out in the middle of a room where it's like a somber fellow making electronic judgments on you. Odd-shaped TV sets make a lot of sense; a tall skinny sliver of a TV set can actually spruce up a dying sitcom. But don't make the mistake of getting a lot of little tiny sets and scattering them about like leftover snacks. Get one solid-looking Big Guy that you can really dig into.

The prospect of a little TV-viewing section with some throw pillows strewn about and a prominent bowl of shelled walnuts may be dismaying to the urbane Lonely Guy—but its effects are likely to be calming.

Gay Cleaning Fellows

Now that you've got your apartment, who's going to clean it up? Good news in this department. Now that *Chorus Line* is a smash and has spawned international companies, there are a lot of dancers who couldn't get into any of them and have become gay cleaning guys. They aren't that easy to find. It isn't as if they advertise conspicuously under names like Joan Crawford Clean-Up and play selections from *Gypsy* on their answering services. They are usually under an Italian name like Fuccione and Calabrese.

Yet such a macho-sounding company can send over a bright-eyed and cheery gay guy with a handkerchief on his head. The best thing about gay cleaning fellows is that they are not afraid of ovens. They go right after them, all the way to the back end, sponging up the last droplet of lamb chop grease. Gay cleaning fellows also know all about the latest cleaning stuff: you may have to take a little ribbing about not having Lemon Pledge Dusting Wax for your breakfront. On the plus side, though, they are considerate enough to Leave the Windex to You, the only fun part in all of cleaning. The only gay cleaning fellows to be wary of are ones from East Germany who may try to Cross That Line. Unless you don't mind waking up on a Sunday morning to a gay cleaning fellow named Wolfgang who has already started on *The New York Times* Arts and Leisure Section.

Cleaning for Poverty-Stricken Lonely Guys

Some Lonely Guys are needy,* and have to clean up their own apartments. If that's your situation, wait till just before company comes and then get down on your knees and roll up all the dust in the room in a big ball. Most of it will come right up, but stubborn dust that refuses to can be dabbed off the floor with a damp palm. Lonely Guys who live around Phoenix and have a sassy Jack Nicholson style may elect to get into dustball fights with another Lonely Guy.

*The state of being in a Negative Cash Flow Situation.

The Big Picture

As a general rule, don't buy anything for your apartment that you can't take along with you. When you batter down a wall to give it an ecclesiastical grotto effect, you may be supplying a free ecclesiastical grotto effect to the next Lonely Guy. Only the strictest interpretation of Maimonides (a biblical Lonely Guy) requires you to do so. The last thing you want to do is put down roots. At a moment's notice, you should be ready and available to pull up stakes and try your luck at being a Lonely Guy in St. Paul de Vence.

The Lonely Guy's Cookbook

He did not like summer camp as a five-year-old and was embar-rassed because he had a hunch-backed counselor. One day, he ate some turnips and became deathly ill. His mother arrived, concerned, compassionate. When she saw how sick he was, she took him home to recuperate. But as soon as he recovered, she sent him right back to the camp with a note, saying, "Here he is again. And he is not to be given any more turnips."

Everyone knows that eggs are the basic Lonely Guy's food. Four in the morning, all alone, throw on some eggs, delicious. But what happens when eggs have lost their charm? When one plate of sunnysides blends unhappily into the next? What happens when the Lonely Guy is egged out?

This is a cookbook for the Lonely Guy who is ready to move Beyond Eggs.

There won't be any braising in this cookbook. Lonely Guys would rather fight than braise. Nor will you be called upon to julienne or mince. In the darkest of all circum-stances, there may be a little dicing, but that's about it. No dredging, no rendering. The Lonely Guy is in no position to put in long hours rendering fat.

What you will find is a modest game plan for nourish-ment which the Lonely Guy must think about if he has some tattered idea of surviving. Several general approaches to cooking will be suggested, along with a few ideas for dishes that will stick to your ribs. Follow these simple procedures and stick to your ribs they will.

Measuring Things

Forget about measuring things. Just tear off hunks of things and toss them in. Lonely Guys are too upset to be dealing with 1½ tsps. of nutmeg which they won't have around anyway.

Diet, Cholesterol, That Stuff

Forget about diet, cholesterol, that stuff. As a Lonely Guy, you deserve only delicious things, even when they are on the fat side. You need all the strength you can get. And remember that *no diet anything tastes good.* Have you tried the new skinny sodas? *Yccchhh!* So get only fat sodas, raspberry and black cherry, the ones you forgot about. They keep them over in the corner. As a Lonely Guy, you will be aggravated a lot and this in itself will tend to keep your weight down. (There will be mornings when you wake up with a sinking feeling and won't want to eat anything at all. That's good for shearing off a few pounds a month right there.)

Eat only incontestably wonderful things—salami, whipped butter. Better to Be a Fat Lonely Guy Than Never to etc., etc. But don't overdo it. Nobody Loves a Dead Fat Lonely Guy. So that you don't become one of those, try to eat a skinny thing every time you eat a fat one. Follow up pizza with a radish. After fried chicken, take a few swallows of grapefruit juice. The fat thing clogs up your arteries and the skinny thing opens them right up for traffic. They've got studies on that. You will practically be able to feel the fat and skinny things fighting it out inside your body.

Daring in the Kitchen

Don't be too daring in the kitchen. For example, don't suddenly get involved with shallots. Later, when you are no longer a Lonely Guy, you can do shallots. Not now. If you know coriander, stay with coriander and don't fool around. Even with coriander you're on thin ice, but at least you've got a shot because it's familiar. Stay with safe things, like pepper.

How Women Can Help

Get a cooking tip from every woman you either have an affair with or have been married to. Every woman has one such terrific tip. A single bay leaf in liver and onions. Putting not only salt but sugar, too, in the vegetables before you cook them. That may be all you got out of a ten-year marriage—putting sugar in the vegetables—but it's something. A pinch of curry in the salad dressing—these tips start to add up, especially if you fool around a lot. And each tip will remind you of the old affair. Every time you sprinkle Tabasco sauce on a sardine sandwich, it will bring back Karen Feinschreiber.

Shortening

Forget about shortening. Nobody really knows what it is.

Leftovers

Somewhere along the line, you will meet a schoolteacher who will tell you to wrap up your leftovers in Baggies.* What a treat it will be to come across them a few days later when you least expect it. This is not true. What you will

*Baggies can also be used for getting your shoes into your galoshes. Stick a Baggie on, and the shoe will slide right in. But that's it for the Baggie. Don't forget yourself and wrap a ham sandwich in a Baggie that's been used for galoshes. Unless you're sure it's been turned inside out.

come across are little piles of old coleslaw which are taking on lives of their own. So when you've had enough to eat, *throw everything out*. Dumping half a western omelet will lift your spirits. You may be a Lonely Guy, but the last thing you want to be is an Unclassy Lonely Guy.

Veal

Veal is the quintessential Lonely Guy meat. There is something pale and lonely about it, especially if it doesn't have any veins. It's so wan and Kierkegaardian. You just know it's not going to hurt you. So eat a lot of veal.

Veal is gentle and benign and can be used in combination with any number of items—peppers, sausages, tomatoes, etc. But veal has its limits. Don't push veal. Don't mix it in with peppermints, for example, and expect to come up with much.

The Big Three

Start every dinner by sautéing onions, peppers and mushrooms in Filippo Berio olive oil. Nothing tastes bad if it starts off with those three. You can then proceed with fish, or chicken—it's not important. Or say you're dashing back and forth between the kitchen and *The Bionic Woman,* trying to decide if Lindsay Wagner has tits. You might just decide to wolf down the onions, peppers and mushrooms and go with Wagner.

The Philosophy of Chicken

You will be working a lot with chicken. The main thing about chicken is the size. Many supermarkets sell giant wings and breasts that scare the hell out of you. They seem to have been hacked off a chicken on the run. A case for L.A. coroner Thomas Noguchi. So get smaller pieces,

although not *too* small because then you're into a whole
dwarf freak-out. You can also buy clean pressed-down slabs
of white-meat chicken, although these seem to have been
bought in an office-supply store and bear little relation to
the crazy barnyard animals you once knew and loved.

Additional Chicken Insights

Before you fry chicken, take the skin off. Lonely Guys don't
realize you're allowed to do that. They think there's some
agreement that the skin stays with the chicken right down to
the wire. You're allowed to rip it right off. It doesn't hurt the
chicken either. The chicken is way past that. If you're cooking the chicken in the oven, pour some honey on it. This tastes
delicious and does not make you a gay Lonely Guy.

A Shocker of a Tip

Don't be too quick to throw in the towel on burned stuff.
Some burned stuff tastes great. Burned French toast, burned
string beans, if you remembered to put a lot of butter on
them. This does not mean burned through and through, big-
time burned. If it's cremated, get rid of it. We are discuss-
ing burned where there is still some good stuff left. Burned
around the edges but not in the middle. If it's major-league
burned, remember to throw out the pot, too, because the
last thing you want to be is a Lonely Guy using Brillo.

A Man on Base

Buy things that are already cooked and almost delicious.
This will give you a Culinary Man on Base. All you have to
do is come in and hit a long fly ball. Don't, for example, do
spaghetti sauce from the gun. If you do, you might as well
have married that Pier Angeli look-alike you found in the
ruins of Sicily while you were with the Occupying Army.
Then you would really be a Lonely Guy because you would

have grown and she wouldn't have. Buy an *existing* spaghetti
sauce—they keep them bland for old folks—and start heaving things in. Onions, cucumbers, garlic—anything im-
proves spaghetti sauce unless it's something freaky like
melon balls. (You can even throw in melon balls if you're in
certain areas north of San Francisco.)

Other Items to Buy That Will Give You a Man on Base

- Cooked lobster, served cold. All you have to throw
  on is lemon and cocktail sauce.
- Bean soup. You hardly have to throw anything in
  except maybe hot dogs. You can throw in lentil
  soup, too.
- Potato pirogies. Throw on any spice you can get
  your hands on.

A Basic Lonely Guy Breakfast

A bagel, strawberries and coffee prepared in a Mr. Coffee
machine. Where are the eggs? You've had your Lonely Guy
eggs at four in the morning with Sinatra music. You've had
a sort of pre-breakfast. And you don't want to do any cooking till later on. The bagel will have a nice crispy wake-up
taste to it. The strawberries are almost ridiculously healthy.
This breakfast will tend to make you think of Chaim Potok
and Beverly Hills, but eat it every day. Once in a while you
can eat nectarines instead of strawberries. But do not make
any substitutions for the bagel.

Table Settings

Grit your teeth and set the table for one, no matter how
excruciating and lonely a process this is. Otherwise you will
have a tendency to eat the whole thing while you're
crouched over the sink. Another thing to grit your teeth

and do is clean up quickly, perhaps after you've had your first bite. If you wake up the next day and see an old half-eaten salmon croquette, it's liable to push you Beyond Loneliness into Forget-About-It City, a place where you don't want to be. Make sure to throw out beer cans, unless you live in the back of a diner, in which case they will fit in with the decor. After a while, a girl named Alma will come and take them away.

A custom at dinner parties is for the host to Present the Table, gather all the guests around the Buffet and introduce each dish. "This is the *saumon fumé,* this is the *Escargots à la Provençale.*" As a goof, and to cut through the gloom, try Presenting the Table to yourself one night. Stand alongside your supper and say aloud: "This is the salami, this is the mustard, this is the rye bread, this is the cherry soda." Then give yourself a brief round of applause and, after a big guffaw, sit down and dig in.

Frozen Milky Ways

Keep a handful in the freezer. You'd be surprised at all the times you're going to want one. Only watch yourself, because Loneliness loosens teeth. There may be studies on that.

A Basic Lonely Guy Lunch

Turkey leg, a pickle and cream soda. You can eat this every day, too, only make sure not to take any phone calls because you will grease up the receiver.

Smell Everything

This is important because certain food-store operators may spot you as a Lonely Guy and use you to try to lay off a marginal slice of flounder.

Things are usually done when they smell good. Wait for

the good smell, then pounce on it and start your eating. This
almost always works.

Refrigerator Tips

Try to have a refrigerator with more than one shelf in
it. Otherwise everything will soon get all lumped together
like in a duffel bag; at the end of the year, you'll find a lot
of boxes of fish sticks and wonder what to do with them.

Liver

The best thing about liver is how virtuous it makes you
feel after you've eaten some. People won't admit it, but they
feel that somehow it connects onto their own liver. There
are no studies to support this. Eat some anyway. If you are
cooking some bacon, you can make a last-minute decision
to throw a few slices of liver in the pan. The bacon will kill
the taste of the liver, and this will get rid of your liver-eating
obligation for some time.

Salad Dressing

Every supermarket has a terrific Italian woman who lives
nearby, bottles her own salad dressing and sells a few dozen
to the supermarket. You'll find them near the okra. These are
great because the Italian woman has not gotten cocky yet. As
a result, her stuff is thick and full of garlic. She has to try
harder, etc. Once Angela gets franchised it will be all over.

The Myth of the Caesar Salad

Caesar salad is a salad that has been made to seem com-
plicated but isn't. They say you need romaine lettuce, but
you don't. Any lettuce will do. You want to go with a
crunchier lettuce, go with it. Then it's oil, vinegar, a raw

egg, cheese, anchovies, lemon juice, garlic, you know the type of thing. *And big croutons.* That's the key. Little ones crumble up and feel like the beach at East Hampton. On the other hand, don't use giant croutons. The Crouton That Took over St. Louis. Then you'll be eating a giant crouton with little dribbly gardens of Caesar salad hanging off it; there's no need to do that.

Crab Boil

Sounds like the worst thing ever invented. Smell it, though, and you'll see that it's slightly fascinating. Figure out something to throw it on. Shrimp is a possibility. A car engine. Anything. Keep crab boil in the back of your mind.

Equipment

- A lot of giant frying pans.
- A chopper. Try to get one that doesn't make you spend all your time digging the chopped stuff off the chopper.
- Terrific-looking knives. Easier said than done. Salesladies will refuse to sell a Lonely Guy the knives he wants, claiming that the coating will come off in the dishwasher. Only skinny, terrible-looking knives will keep their coating. *Don't fall for this.* Insist on the terrific-looking ones. Even when the coating washes off, they look better than the ones that keep their coating. If you live in a densely populated urban center, you'll be able to slip a few of your knives into your coat pocket when you have to run downstairs for things you've forgotten.
- A lot of sponges for grape-juice stains. Lonely Guys spill a lot of grape juice.

Garlic

One of the great treats about being a Lonely Guy is you can use all the garlic you like since "who cares?" Use it on everything except Rice Krispies and melon balls. Just for the fun of it, run into a delicatessen and holler out the French name for garlic: *Aiiieee.*

A treat for garlic-lovers is Slow-Cooked Garlic Chicken. This is not a dish in which the chicken is cooked in a slothful and heavy-footed manner. It means dousing the chicken with garlic and cooking it for a long time, an hour and a half or so, at a temperature of 280 degrees. In that manner, the garlic will penetrate to every part of the chicken, under the arms, the feet, everywhere. No part of that chicken is safe from this garlic onslaught which is what you've always wanted in your dreams.

Pounding

The butcher does this. Some people think it means putting their meat into tidy one-pound packages. It doesn't. It means taking the fight out of it. Don't let your butcher do it. As a Lonely Guy, the last thing you need to see is meat that's been beaten into submission and lost its will to survive.

Meatballs

Unless you've got a lot of time on your hands, there is no way to keep meatballs round and bouncy.* Eggs won't do it. Neither will bread crumbs. Only compounds developed in the

---

*One suggested method is to slip them into the freezer, half an hour before cooking. Unless your timing is exquisite, and you snatch them out of there just in time, you'll wind up with little meatsicles that have no real function.

space program have a chance of keeping meatballs round. So
be prepared to have them go to pieces on you. As a Lonely
Guy, it may not be pleasant for you to see a meatball go to
pieces. Take comfort in the fact that even meatballs that have
come apart at the seams can be reasonably delicious.

A Basic Dinner: Lonely Guy Veal Parmigiana à la Tomate

Quickly eat some lettuce with Roquefort dressing. Your
salad will be out of the way and you won't have to worry
about it.

Have a drink. Stolichnaya Vodka with Clamato. It's all
right to keep Stolichnaya Vodka in the freezer because of its
low freezing point. And if they are wrong and it freezes, hack
off a piece and drink it when it thaws out. If you are in a
hurry, suck it.

Take the veal out of the wrapper, the veal that you haven't
allowed the butcher to pound into submission. Put it where
you can find it, against a dark background, since it's pale
and will tend to disappear on you.

Have your second Stolichnaya Vodka with Clamato.

Get the Big Three going in Berio olive oil. Put it in your
biggest frying pan.

Try to find the veal. If you come up with it, squoosh it
around in a mixture of eggs and crumbled-up corn flakes.
Hold on tight and make sure it doesn't slip out of your hands.
Otherwise, you will lose it down the drain. A lot of great
veal has been lost that way. Get the veal going in another
big frying pan.

Try to keep your nerves steady, because you are about to
do a *third* thing. Only Lonely Guys who have been chopper
pilots in Nam will be able to stay calm at this point. Put
some existing tomato sauce in a pot and start heaving things
in—every spice you can come up with. Remember, though,
that bay leaves tend to take over.

Somehow, get all of this together—the veal, the tomato sauce, the Big Three—in one giant frying pan as big as a football field. (Don't get all excited and squirt Right Guard in the pan; Lonely Guys often keep Right Guard in the kitchen.)

Lay strips of mozzarella cheese on the veal. Turn the oven up to four hundred degrees, set the whole creation in the oven and run like a sonofabitch.

Have a glass of wine. You can use some from a leftover bottle. It does not lose its body. That's all a myth designed to get you to buy lots of wine. Leftover wine has a pleasingly sullen taste to it.

Take careful peeks into the oven, making sure to crane your head in another direction so that the oven doesn't explode on you. When the dish looks the way things look in reliable neighborhood Italian restaurants, take it out and plunge in.

To be fair to this dish, it must be eaten when it's hot enough to sear the roof of your mouth.

This recipe can be used with chicken, meatballs or fish, although fish will make it a little boring.

Backup Restaurants

In the middle of cooking, you may suddenly slump over, unable to continue. For this reason, it's good to have some late-night backup restaurants that serve bacon cheeseburgers and Chinese food. It is important that these restaurants be festive, because when you arrive you're going to be down three touchdowns. They should have at least a handful of women around who are known to be "sure things."

Having People Over

The only reason to have someone over is so that she will feel sorry for you when she sees that none of your dishes match. When you bring out your glasses—leftover from three-in-a-carton shrimp cocktails—it will break her heart. Within a week, she will send over a complete set of dishes and a chopper. Be careful, though. She will try to end your Lonely Guy status, which you don't want to do quite yet.

Good luck to you in your life as a reasonably well fed Lonely Guy.

Grooming

The father had lived through many great and turbulent events in history—the outbreak of World War One, the Lindbergh Kidnapping. Hitler's March into Poland. Roosevelt's Fourth term, man's first walk on the moon. The Phenomenon that amazed him the most, however, took place each morning when his son would get up, put on his pants, tighten the belt and then try to stuff his shirt in through the belt. He never could get over that.

Who cares how I look, the Lonely Guy will ask. My grocer? Why should I take the trouble to smell nice? Is there a line around the block waiting to smell me? All I ever do is slip around corners. Do I have to be well-groomed to do that? In sum, why should I be a Well-Groomed Lonely Guy?

These are sound questions. And there *is* a case to be made for bad grooming. (You don't have to do anything. You just lie there and vegetate, etc.)

But remember: Good grooming eats away at the clock, that scourge of the Lonely Guy. Taking showers, opening up tight mouthwash bottles, trying to get anchovy paste stains off a shirt—all this can kick the hell out of a day. Before you know it, a week is gone. Ask any Lonely Guy what an advantage that is.

Good grooming can fake people into thinking you are not in agony. This is a good thing. If people ever realized how lousy you felt, they simply would not stand for it, the way they couldn't take Bangladesh. They would break down doors in an effort to rid you of your Loneliness, which, of course, is all you've got going.

With minimal effort, the Lonely Guy can be almost as well-groomed as a normal person. One example should suffice: Many Lonely Guys cut their toenails and don't bother to catch them up in anything. They take no responsibility for them whatever, allowing them to fly all over the place. The Well-Groomed Lonely Guy keeps an ashtray alongside his feet, like a target, and lets the toenails carom off this. A *p-i-n-n-n-g* sound results which is not altogether unpleasant. From this point on, it's a simple matter to collect the toenails and get them the hell out of there. You won't be able to trap every last one. Is anyone saying that you will? But let's say you get eight out of ten. That's eight toenails you won't have to worry about again. Hats off and goodbye. No nightmares about a cute girl's picking up a handful and saying, "What the hell are these?"

The Smell of Loneliness

Let's face it, Lonely Guys have a smell of their own. You've read about it in novels. "Axel had a smell of loneliness about him." It's not bitter or acrid or anything, but it *is* a little stale, like an old herringbone suit. Nothing much can be done about it. It's socked all the way in there. But the Lonely Guy has a responsibility to himself and to the community to go after that smell. That means taking plenty of showers. Generally speaking, the Lonely Guy should avoid baths. It hardly requires pointing out here that an occasional Lonely Guy, snug and secure in a warm tub, will decide to stay right where he is, packing it in, then and there. Contrarily, there is no known instance of someone deciding to end it all in a shower, by, say, getting up on his toes and smacking his head against the nozzle.

Any sweet-smelling soap will do, though preferably not one that's so slippery you have to keep chasing after it. Some Lonely Guys have reported results from a dab of dishwasher detergent. The most important thing about soap is not to save up a whole bunch of skinny leftover pieces of it. Many an affluent Lonely Guy, who would think nothing of buying a Ferrari, will turn right around and start saving little pieces of soap. Or worse, try to mash them together to make a new bar out of them. When it gets around three-quarters of the way down, throw the soap away and accept your loss graciously. Each time you start a new bar, you will experience a clean Born Again feeling.

While any soap will do, that's not quite the case with shampoos. One of the biggest mistakes a Lonely Guy can ever make is to buy a tar shampoo. Admittedly, it will make his hair smell fresh and outdoorsy. But it may also make him feel he is wandering around in the woods somewhere, lonelier than ever. Worse, it might conjure up thoughts of fall, the hardest of all seasons for the Lonely Guy to get through, each falling leaf a stake in his heart. (Summer, when everyone else is going away, isn't so wonderful for him either. Neither, for that matter, is winter, when the whole world is out there playing with snowmobiles and he isn't. The best time for the Lonely Guy seems to be a two-week span at the end of March when not much is going on.)

Before leaving the shower, feel around and make sure to pull out the hairs that get caught in the drain. No one is saying you have to do this after every single shower. But don't make the mistake of many Lonely Guys and let it pile up so that it has to be trucked out of there.

Make sure your towels are not only fluffy but large. What's the point of having a towel if it will only dry one knee? You'd be surprised at all the Lonely Guys who will use thirteen tiny little towels for a single shower. So use a big towel, but not one that's so huge you feel lost and abandoned in it. Some Lonely Guys like to warm up their towels, like dinner rolls.

This is all right, so long as you don't drape them over a toaster. They can be heated up on a radiator or even put in the oven, but don't get carried away and throw a grilled cheese sandwich in there, too.

Just because a towel is a little dirty in one place is no reason it has to be rushed over to the laundry. There may be other places where it's still a little clean. Lots of other places. When these are used up, it *still* doesn't have to go to the laundry. A cute girl can be invited over to take a shower and to use the suspect towel. When she's gone, the towel will smell fresh and pretty again; you will be amazed and delighted to see how many showers it has left in it.

Talcum powder is excellent for after-shower grooming so long as you don't snort or swallow it. There is no known antidote for swallowed talcum powder. The Lonely Guy who has it in him will have to resign himself to a life with powdered internal organs.

In selecting a deodorant, the Lonely Guy should pass up the roll-on type and go after the spray variety. The reason for this is that the Lonely Guy usually forgets about the deodorant until his shirt is on. It's much easier to spray right through the shirt than it is to try to get the roll-on up through the sleeve until it makes contact with the armpit. And don't be afraid to spray a little underarm deodorant someplace else, on your feet, for example. This is not an arrestable offense. "All right, men . . . put the cuffs on him. Guess where he put underarm deodorant. . . ."

Many Lonely Guys who were bearded through the social upheaval of the Sixties have now returned to shaving, only to run into that same old puzzle—how to deal with the Adam's apple. Most Lonely Guys have a prominent one, as a result of having to gulp down so much bad news. The Adam's apple is the most delicate part of a man's body. For this reason, it makes no sense to keep nipping off the end of it. Lonely Guys with responsible dads learned early in the game that there is only one way to go at an Adam's apple:

Pinch the skin out, swing it to one side, shave, then swing
it back the other way, and shave again. Simple enough. But
how many Lonely Guys have reached the age of forty and
have been in the dark about this technique? How many, to
this day, wear turtlenecks to cover up a hairy Adam's apple?

To stop the flow of blood caused by shaving gashes, many
Lonely Guys use little dabs of toilet paper which they stick
on there. The main drawback is that they often forget to
take them off and have to be pulled aside at parties and
told about them. Short of a strangulating tourniquet, the
best way to stop up a shaving gash remains the styptic
pencil, one of the few constants in American life. It is the
only item in Western civilization to have undergone no
technological breakthrough. During the long years of early
space exploration, many of us here on the ground wondered
how it would benefit the styptic pencil. The answer, sad
to say, is that it didn't.

The Lonely Guy who has finished up shaving will be well
advised to check his nose hairs and consider trimming them
back. Not after every shave. Not even once a week, necessarily. But at some point. Does it make any sense to wait
till you're tripping over them? No. A sign posted in the foyer
saying "Trim Back Nose Hairs" may offend a guest or two
but will serve as a reminder of this important grooming step.

Brief Fashion Analysis for
the Lonely Guy

It isn't important that the Lonely Guy plan his outfits days
in advance or slave over the coordination of his colors. But
it's nice for him to have a "look." This can be pulled off with
a single identifying trademark—a peaked cap, a maroon
windbreaker, or even an old college T-shirt that he wears—
rain or shine.

The clothes-conscious Lonely Guy may also want to have
a suit made for special occasions. This will require many trips

to the tailor so that his measurements can be established on grid lines and properly hooked up to a satellite. Then, the Lonely Guy can order suits from anywhere on the globe and have the fun of saying:

"Hi, I'm Tom Henderson. Get out my grid lines. I'd like to order a suit; I'm calling from here in Damascus."

It's a waste of money to have shirts made to order—except for the measurement that gives you room enough to slide your watch *under* the cuff—so you don't have to jam your cuff under the watchband.

Oral Hints

To ensure excellent breath, a good mouthwash is recommended. The Lonely Guy with Dragon Mouth is not going to get very far in life. One way to tell if your mouthwash is too strong is to see if you can still taste liverwurst. However, some Lonely Guys have given up mouthwash and gone over to liverwurst. Up in the morning, mouth a little stale, cut a slice of liverwurst, wash it down with Clamato and you're in business.

An amazing number of Lonely Guys go through their lives in terrible fear of swallowing toothpaste. This is ridiculous. What kind of life is that! It *could* put you out of business, but you would have to wolf down tube after tube of it and who's going to take the time to do that? So pick out a more reasonable fear, for heaven's sake.

Cologne Again, Naturally

It's essential that the Lonely Guy select just the right cologne. Sounds easy, but it's hard to tell what a cologne is like if you're the one it's on. Many Lonely Guys choose their cologne on the basis of the bottle.

"That's quite a bottle. These cologne guys must know something about cologne."

Another way to look at it is if they've spent all that money on a great bottle, there was probably no money left for the cologne. Or they're using a wonderful bottle to pass off a crappy cologne. But this is the Conspiracy approach to American life again, coming back to haunt us, and it should probably be kept out of colognes. Think in between. Choose a nice-looking bottle.* But don't insist that it be carved out of stained glass by Dominican friars.

One way to check out a cologne is to put some on, walk out of the room and then dash back in and smell the place you were. Another is the time-honored Elevator Test. Apply the cologne and step into a crowded elevator at noontime. If the other passengers huddle in a corner and begin to swat the air in front of them, you may be on the wrong track. If they shift from one foot to the other, but steadily hold their ground, you are probably in the clear.

Once you've selected a cologne, stick to it. Don't put one cologne on your face and another on your feet, totally confusing the person who is smelling you. And stay away from colognes that are too macho and make you want to kick everyone in the stomach.

Beyond the Shower

The Lonely Guy must not only keep himself clean but also look after the clothing that he wears. His best friend in this department is Woolite, which can get any item in the world Slightly Clean. This product has virtually put dry cleaners out of business. When shown a container of Woolite, many have been known to punch out at it. To use Woolite, put your dirty clothes in a sinkful of cold water, sprinkle some

---

*Some of the best colognes are the ones in frosted bottles at the barber shop. (They look like Gilbey's gin bottles.) But you've actually got to *be* a barber to own one of those.

in and let everything soak for around three minutes. It's that cold water that gets people suspicious. How can you get stuff clean with cold water! Everyone's a little shaky on the answer, but what seems to happen is that the dirt gets cold. And cold dirt doesn't seem to smell as bad as hot dirt. Something like that. In any case, it's important to make your return to the sink in three minutes. Clothes left overnight in Woolite tend to rot away when you're wearing them at parties. Don't worry about getting all the Woolite squeezed out of the clothing. Woolite itself has a nice smell and can be used as an emergency cologne. Now, only every six months or so will you have to take your clothing to the laundry. Lonely Guys have been known to buy cabins in Vermont with the money they saved on Woolite. They become lonelier than ever once they do that—but that's another story.

Quite often the Lonely Guy will have a favorite leather jacket that doesn't smell so hot after a while. No amount of Woolite can get through to it. For this situation, there is a special process called Deep Steam-Cleaning which penetrates right through to the DNA structure of the jacket and makes it sweet-smelling again. This process costs as much as a Toyota, but it is worth it to the Lonely Guy who only feels secure in that one favorite jacket.

Buttons, too, are best left for the dry cleaner. No Lonely Guy should ever attempt to sew one on. When he tries and fails to thread the needle, he will be reminded of the erosion of his capacities, his decline and eventual you-know-what. Once the first button has fallen off something, it's safe to assume that all the others will follow. Sewing them back on one at a time is like trying to shore up the Thieu Regime. When the first one goes, cut bait and take them over to the dry cleaner; he will machine-sew them on so that they will still be standing there—like the British Empire—long after the shirt has fallen apart.

The Chinese Laundry

A word about Chinese laundries. Isn't it time we took a hard look at them? After all these years, they still insist they didn't put starch in your collar—even if you crack off a piece of collar and eat it right on the spot. Quietly they've sneaked up the prices which are now on a par with Gold Coast Cleaners, right down the block. Many a Lonely Guy has gotten into financial hot water by going on expensive vacations, thinking he's saved all that money by using Chinese laundries—when he hasn't saved a dime.

If one of your shirts comes back with a sleeve gone, suddenly all they know how to talk is Chinese. Worst of all is that skinny string they put on bundles which gives you finger and palm gashes. Many feel that this is their way of undermining the Western democracies—but this is probably going too far. Don't feel you are smoothing over Chinese-American relations by continuing to use their laundries. Leave that kind of thing to the Secretary of State.

Be firm with your Chinese laundry. Maybe if we all become Chinese laundry hard-liners, we can get them to give out free litchi nuts again.

A Trio of Grooming Tips

Shoe Polish. Many Lonely Guys let their shoes get dirty because they're afraid to get polish on their cuffs. This is absurd. Polish on the cuffs can actually be an advantage, serving as a fashion segue to your shoes. Something new in color coordination. On the other hand, getting polish on the hands is a legitimate fear since it must be removed surgically.

Food Stains. Almost every Lonely Guy makes the mistake of trying to get food stains off, which, of course, usually makes the problem worse. Say you're dealing with marinara sauce on a shirt. Moisten the towel, dab it on the trouble spot and slowly rub the towel around in an ever-broadening circle so that the entire shirt is covered with a light marinara sauce hue. This is better than having just one conspicuous marinara sauce spot.

Putting Things Away. On occasion, the Lonely Guy will wake up with a sinking feeling that's worse than the one he usually has. He can't figure out what's wrong with him. The answer may be a simple one. He has a lot of old gray T-shirts lying around. Nothing is more depressing than seeing this. For a feeling of well-being, put things away. Stick your dirty socks in a drawer with the clean ones; it's not important. You'll worry about this later. The main thing is to get them out of sight.

In sum, try to look and smell as nice as possible. Remember, the clean, well-groomed Lonely Guy is a Lonely Guy better able to face the future, no matter how peculiar that future may be.

Lonely Guy on the Run

His best sport was tennis. He had a slashing, almost mystical fore-
hand. At a Midwestern college, he took on all comers, defeating All-
American types named Bryce and Jamie. After a year of this, he
laid down his racket and never played again. He felt certain that
a legend would spring up about a slender mysterious boy from the
East who almost magically pulverized everyone in sight and then
disappeared. But no legend sprung up. He kept checking, but as far
as he knew, no one ever mentioned him again.

One of your main problems as a Lonely Guy is energy. Not President Carter's kind. The other kind. Where
on earth are you going to get some? One answer is running.
Even if you have to drag yourself out there to do it, you'll
wind up healthier than you were.

Running is basically a Lonely Guy activity. If you doubt
it, go out and run and start waving to people running toward you and see what happens. No one will wave back. The
only ones to respond at all will be people who are curious
about everything that moves.

As a runner, you've got to go it alone.

What it Does for Your Body

One of the wonderful things about running is what it does
for your body. Your belly will gradually get whittled down

until it's small and hard and round. Unfortunately, it won't go away completely, but will remain in the form of a hard little volleyball of a belly. Running will also give you sloping shoulders and a thin haunted appearance which is irresistible to Finns. Don't be surprised if you develop a high adenoidal whine, like someone who was tortured in Algeria.

Some of the fat that gets pared down may tend to collect in the form of high, billowing steatopygic buttocks, common to Zulu warriors. Make sure you're not one of the fellows that happens to.

Tough Feet

Make sure you have tough feet. Practice on little piles of gravel. Distance running has been called a tribute to the indomitable human spirit when actually it's a tribute to human feet. Many people don't make it in running because their feet are quitters. They are willing to go on, but their feet always want to throw in the towel. All the great marathon runners* had wonderful feet. If you could shine a flashlight on Frank Shorter's** feet at midnight, you'd see that he has better ones than anyone else, that he actually has unfair feet and in a sense runs a spitter.

What to Wear

The proper outfit for running is a department store track suit with a single stripe on it so that cars don't crash into you. These outfits are inching up in price. Some of them cost more

---

*Every runner dreams of entering the Boston Marathon but doesn't do it for fear of coming in last. "And now, in position number 6000 . . . Mr. George Kreevy." So what if you're last! Look at Phil Jackson. Nobody's first choice for the NBA Hall of Fame. Yet nothing was wrong with him.

**U.S. Gold Medal winner for Marathon, 1972.

than real suits and are nice enough to wear to discotheques. Don't get an overfancy running suit that's covered with fluorescent stripes, though, or you'll look like a roadblock.

If you wear shorts, make sure they are trim and not the bouffant type. Don't wear shorts at all if you have white hairy legs. (Don't run around *naked*. Just cover up those legs.)

A jockstrap is recommended so long as you don't keep snapping it in irritation when you're not having a good run. See that your socks are even in height or you will make the runner in back of you seasick. It's all right if your socks are a little gray. Knowledgeable runners know that gray socks are not necessarily filthy and might even be a little clean by Lonely Guy standards. Wear sneakers that are comfortable, even if they are for another sport. It's not an arrestable offense to run in squash sneakers. They don't immediately pull you over. All that stuff about special sneakers for punchball, or special rowing sneakers, was started by the sneaker bigwigs so that a person would be embarrassed if he didn't own at least forty pairs.

It's offensive to run while fully dressed, wearing business shoes and socks that have little clocks on them. Don't be one of those guys.

On Your Way to Running

Lonely Guys who live in the city will have to run past stores and buildings to get to wherever it is they're going to do their running. Along the way, doormen and supermarket checkout guys will needle you by running along with you for a while. Just ignore them and take it in a good-natured way. Otherwise, they will stay with you, and there's nothing more embarrassing than to run for miles with a supermarket checkout guy matching you stride for stride.

When you're standing on the corner in your shorts, waiting for the light to change, don't shift your weight from one foot to the other or you'll be arrested as a hooker.

A Philosophy of Running

It's terribly important to develop a Philosophy of Running. What you've got to do is eliminate all feelings of competitiveness and just run for the feeling of health and well-being. Since this is impossible, the next best thing is Beating Guys. This is not as easy as it sounds. There are not that many guys around you can beat. Fat Guys are misleading since a lot of them have piston-like power in their haunches. Catholic High School Guys are out of the question. No one can catch those driven Kennedy look-alikes. And you can forget about fellows from Eastern Europe since every last one of them can run like a sonofabitch. Even Czech filmmakers who take a lot of quaaludes are fast runners. Is there any need to get into Asians? Occasionally, you can beat a Young Guy who is just out there a few times out of guilt from Singles' Bar attendance. You can always beat a bartender.

Once you see that you can beat a guy, you might as well beat him twice and get that the hell out of the way once and for all. The way to do that is to pass him, then slow down as if you're out of gas. When he passes you, start running full out again and Beat Him a Second Time. That will really crush his spirit and you should have no trouble with him in the future. When you've passed him that second time, it's excessive to raise your arms victoriously and sing "Feelin' Free Now" from *Rocky*.

Actual Running

When you're actually out there running, the proper technique is to lift your feet just far enough off the ground so that no one can accuse you of walking. Bouncing along vigorously on your toes looks good but is death on your arches and should only be used to impress girls. Or to spring out of the wings for an *Annie* audition. Don't throw punches at the sky or someone will walk up and start fighting with you.

Take little tiny breaths and make sure no air gets into your lungs, especially if you are running in the city. In fact, do as little breathing as possible. If you have to do a lot of breathing, wait till you get home. Do you want your lungs to look like an old Chevrolet?

Getting it Over With

For all of its attractive features, running does tend to get a little boring. So one of your main objectives is how to get the damned thing over with as fast as possible. Along these lines, don't pay any attention to how far you're going or how long it takes you to get there. Otherwise you'll be all caught up in mathematical computations. Just run toward something, an old lady who sits in the same place every day.* When you reach her, there is no reason to sit down with her and get involved with her life. Just turn around, or tap her if you have to, and start back the other way. If she is not there, do not panic and go looking for her in the neighborhood. She'll be all right.

One way to make the time pass quickly is to lose yourself in thoughts of space and eternity and the nature of the universe. This is usually more boring than running. Another thing to do is write a musical comedy in your head. This will make you run faster since you'll want to get back and see how it shapes up on paper. Still another time-killing device is to make up Academy Award acceptance speeches.

The Dangers

Running is a lot more dangerous than you think. People assume it's easy and as a result they're not careful and they

---

*Many of these old folks have their slacks rolled up so that their knees can get sunned. Can sunned knees be the long sought-after key to longevity?

fall down a lot. Sometimes they trip over people who are
lying around in the park. It may not look it, but it's a long
way down, especially if you're a tall guy. The ground is not
as close as it was when you were a kid. Once you see you're
going to fall, go into a roll, taking the blow on your neck,
or someplace like that, spring lightly to your feet and try to
make it to a hospital. If you think you've broken something,
don't move, just lie there in a heap and hope that another
runner will drag you out of sight.

Another danger is guys throwing things down at your
head from overpasses. Don't run after them unless you're sure
you want to catch them.

Chicken-Walkers

Sooner or later, you'll come across a fellow doing an odd
and embarrassing strut that is neither running nor walking but some dreadful hybrid of the two. This is the infa-
mous chicken-walker, the loneliest and most despised man
in all of sports. So named because of his barnyard gait and
the pecking movements of his head. He'll be followed by
a pack of kids yelling "Chicken-walker, chicken-walker."
Don't assume that you're automatically going to turn into
one of these fellows some day. There is no reason why you
have to. If you'd like, you can go into a corner where no
one can see you, and try a little chicken-walking, just to
get it out of your system.

After it's Over

After you've stopped running, don't just stop dead on a
dime. Stop gradually, going into a little trot, the way race-
horses do. But stop eventually. A lot of fellows like to show
off their running by running all over the place, dashing out
of stationery stores, challenging cars to races. No one likes
that kind of fellow.

When you reach your building after a run, you've got to decide how to get up to your apartment. Do you take the stairs or the elevator? Remember, you're soaking wet and even if it's a healthy animal kind of thing, nobody cares. All they know about is sweat.

If you choose the elevator, there is a strong chance that some woman from New Hampshire will order you off. Your best bet is to ask the freight elevator man if you can go up with some umbrella stands.

Once you're home, don't spoil the whole run by drinking everything in sight. The most you should drink is a couple of bottles of cream soda.

Sometime after you run, you'll probably start to get exhausted and want to take a nap. That's all right, but don't be surprised if your sleep is restless. That's because even though you've finished running, your body may not have had its fill and wants to get in some more. Be very careful about this, because during the nap your body may just up and run right out of the apartment.

One of the ways to tell that running is good for you is all the people who will try to get you to stop. A fellow with a perfectly good watch will dart out at you and ask you what time it is. A neighbor in the elevator will warn you that unless you can get your pulse down to around twelve beats a minute you're just wasting your time and may even be destroying yourself. Someone else will insist that you stop running and play tennis. Take a good look at him. He's probably got a mean and cranky face from being on the phone all the time trying to line up partners for doubles and from arguing about whether the ball was on the baseline.

These people do not care about you. They just want you to stop running so you won't be healthier than they are.

Nobody really *enjoys* running. After all, you're not crazy. Even on a cool fall day with a nice nip in the air, it isn't *fun.* It's just not a normal human activity, like sleeping. But once you've finished an exhausting run, and they're all exhausting, you can have the thrill of not having to do it for a while.

So get out there and run—to hit back at all those people who'd love it if you stopped, to feel the joy of getting it over with, and to be a fit Lonely Guy.

Eating Alone in Restaurants

Since money was scarce, their pattern was to order dinners for them-
selves and an "extra plate" for their son, upon which they would
deposit dabs of meat and vegetables. When the boy became center on
his high school basketball team, he rebelled one night at Caruso's
Grill.
"I don't want any more Extra Plates," he said. "I want a din-
ner of my own."
"You're not ready yet," said his mother. "When the time comes,
I'll tell you. And here, take some of my broccoli. I never liked the
stuff here anyway."

Hunched over, trying to be as inconspicuous as possible, a solitary diner slips into a midtown Manhattan steak-
house. No sooner does he check his coat than the voice of
the headwaiter comes booming across the restaurant.
"Alone again, eh?"
As all eyes are raised, the bartender, with enormous good
cheer, chimes in: "That's because they all left him high and
dry."
And then, just in case there is a customer in the restaurant who isn't yet aware of his situation, a waiter shouts out
from the buffet table: "Well, we'll take care of him anyway,
won't we fellas!"

Haw, haw, haw, and a lot of sly winks and pokes in the ribs. Eating alone in a restaurant is one of the most terrifying experiences in America.

Sniffed at by headwaiters, an object of scorn and amusement to couples, the solitary diner is the unwanted and unloved child of Restaurant Row. No sooner does he make his appearance than he is whisked out of sight and seated at a thin sliver of a table with barely enough room on it for an hors d'oeuvre. Wedged between busboy stations, a hairs breadth from the men's room, there he sits, feet lodged in a railing as if he were in Pilgrim stocks, wondering where he went wrong in life.

Rather than face this grim scenario, most Lonely Guys would prefer to nibble away at a tuna fish sandwich in the relative safety of their high-rise apartments.

What can be done to ease the pain of this not only starving but silent minority—to make dining alone in restaurants a rewarding experience? Absolutely nothing. But some small strategies *do* exist for making the experience bearable.

Before You Get There

Once the Lonely Guy has decided to dine alone at a restaurant, a sense of terror and foreboding will begin to build throughout the day. All the more reason for him to get there as quickly as possible so that the experience can soon be forgotten and he can resume his normal life. Clothing should be light and loose-fitting, especially around the neck—on the off chance of a fainting attack during the appetizer. It is best to dress modestly, avoiding both the funeral-director-style suit as well as the bold, eye-arresting costume of the gaucho. A single cocktail should suffice; little sympathy will be given to the Lonely Guy who tumbles in, stewed to the gills. (The fellow who stoops to putting morphine in his toes for courage does not belong in this discussion.) En route to the restaurant, it is best to play down dramatics, such as swinging the arms pluckily and humming the theme from *The Bridge on the River Kwai.*

Once You Arrive

The way your entrance comes off is of critical importance. Do not skulk in, slipping along the walls as if you are carrying some dirty little secret. There is no need, on the other hand, to fling your coat arrogantly at the hatcheck girl, slap the headwaiter across the cheeks with your gloves and demand to be seated immediately. Simply walk in with a brisk rubbing of the hands and approach the headwaiter. When asked how many are in your party, avoid cute responses such as "Jes lil ol' me." Tell him you are a party of one; the Lonely Guy who does not trust his voice can simply lift a finger. Do not launch into a story about how tired you are of taking out fashion models, night after night, and what a pleasure it is going to be to dine alone.

It is best to arrive with no reservation. Asked to set aside a table for one, the restaurant owner will suspect either a prank on the part of an ex-waiter, or a terrorist plot, in which case windows will be boarded up and the kitchen bomb-swept. An advantage of the "no reservation" approach is that you will appear to have just stepped off the plane from Des Moines, your first night in years away from Marge and the kids.

All eyes will be upon you when you make the promenade to your table. Stay as close as possible to the headwaiter, trying to match him step for step. This will reduce your visibility and fool some diners into thinking you are a member of the staff. If you hear a generalized snickering throughout the restaurant, do not assume automatically that you are being laughed at. The other diners may all have just recalled an amusing moment in a Feydeau farce.

If your table is unsatisfactory, do not demand imperiously that one for eight people be cleared immediately so that you can dine in solitary grandeur. Glance around discreetly and see if there are other possibilities. The ideal table will allow you to keep your back to the wall so that you can see if anyone is laughing at you. Try to get one close to another couple so that if you lean over at a 45-degree angle it will appear that you are a swinging member of their group. Sitting opposite a mirror can be useful; after a drink or two, you will begin to feel that there are a few of you.

Once you have been seated, and it becomes clear to the staff that you are alone, there will follow The Single Most Heartbreaking Moment in Dining Out Alone—when the second setting is whisked away and yours is spread out a bit to make the table look busier. This will be done with great ceremony by the waiter—angered in advance at being tipped for only one dinner. At this point, you may be tempted to smack your forehead against the table and curse the fates that brought you to this desolate position in life. A wiser course is to grit your teeth, order a drink and use this opportunity to make contact with other Lonely Guys sprinkled about the room. A menu or a leafy stalk of celery can be used as a shield for peering out at them. Do not expect a hearty greeting or a cry of "huzzah" from these frightened and browbeaten people. Too much excitement may cause them to slump over, curtains. Smile gently and be content if you receive a pale wave of the hand in return. It is unfair to imply that you have come to help them throw off their chains.

When the headwaiter arrives to take your order, do not be bullied into ordering the last of the gazelle haunches unless you really want them. Thrilled to be offered anything at all, many Lonely Guys will say "Get them right out here" and wolf them down. Restaurants take unfair advantage of Lonely Guys, using them to get rid of anything from withered liver to old heels of roast beef. Order anything you like, although it is good to keep to the light and simple in case of a sudden attack of violent stomach cramps.

Some Proven Strategies

Once the meal is under way, a certain pressure will begin to build as couples snuggle together, the women clucking sympathetically in your direction. Warmth and conviviality will pervade the room, none of it encompassing you. At this point, many Lonely Guys will keep their eyes riveted to the restaurant paintings of early Milan or bury themselves in a paperback anthology they have no wish to read.

Here are some ploys designed to confuse other diners and make them feel less sorry for you.

- After each bite of food, lift your head, smack your lips thoughtfully, swallow and make a notation in a pad. Diners will assume you are a restaurant critic.
- Between courses, pull out a walkie-talkie and whisper a message into it. This will lead everyone to believe you are part of a police stakeout team, about to bust the salad man as an international dope dealer.
- Pretend you are a foreigner. This is done by pointing to items on the menu with an alert smile and saying to the headwaiter: "Is good, no?"
- When the main course arrives, brush the restaurant silverware off the table and pull some of your own out of a breast pocket. People will think you are a wealthy eccentric.
- Keep glancing at the door, and make occasional trips to look out at the street, as if you are waiting for a beautiful woman. Halfway through the meal, shrug in a world-weary manner and begin to eat with gusto. The world is full of women! Why tolerate bad manners! Life is too short.

The Right Way

One other course is open to the Lonely Guy, an audacious one, full of perils, but all the more satisfying if you can bring it off. That is to take off your dark glasses, sit erectly, smile broadly at anyone who looks in your direction, wave off inferior wines, and begin to eat with heartiness and enormous confidence. As outrageous as the thought may be—enjoy your own company. Suddenly, titters and sly winks will tail off, the headwaiter's disdain will fade, and friction will build among couples who will turn out to be not as tightly cemented as they appear. The heads of other Lonely Guys will lift with hope as you become the attractive center of the room.

If that doesn't work, you still have your fainting option.

Part Two

Life's Little
Challenges
and Dilemmas

The Worst Lonely Guy Story

After twenty-two years of marriage, a television producer left his family and took temporary lodging in a one-bedroom apartment on the top floor of a high-rise building overlooking Hollywood's Sunset Strip. At midnight, his second day away from home, it was time for him to take his eardrops and he realized he had never put them in without help. He stepped outside; normally, a few hookers stood around in the hallway, but this time there were none in sight. He took the elevator downstairs and explained his predicament to the doorman. Suspicious at first, the doorman agreed to put them in. The producer knelt down on the lobby carpeting and put his head in the doorman's lap, one ear tilted upward. This is the tableau that was picked up on the security monitors. Armed guards flew out and demanded to know what was going on. They listened to his explanation, but even after they returned to their stations, he could tell they were not convinced.

The Lonely Guy
with Temperature

He was the only one of twenty-three boys in his neighborhood who did not become either a doctor, dentist or nurse's aide. One day he met the mother of a childhood friend. She told him of her son's various triumphs as a cardiologist in Louisville, then asked what he was doing.

"Teaching English," he said. "I'm chairman of the department."

"That's the way life is," she said, clutching his arm sympathetically. "You just can't always get what you want out of it."

Illness is a stern test for the Lonely Guy. Most people get subtle warnings before they become ill—feelings of edginess, drift, despair. The Lonely Guy has these feelings all the time, even when he is bursting with health. He must rely on more obvious trouble signs—such as fainting in lobbies and falling out of chairlifts.

No comforting hand will be there to pull the Lonely Guy through an illness. At the first sign of fever, he may panic, and be tempted to scribble off a note: "I had temperature. I just couldn't go on," then quietly phase himself out of the game.

Such drastic behavior is uncalled for.

Today's sick Lonely Guy stands almost as good a chance at recovery as anyone else.

The New Sickness

Sickness may have changed since the last time the Lonely Guy was ill. In the Old Sickness, the Lonely Guy ran a fever and the family sat around waiting for it to "break." Either it did or it didn't. In the latter case, he was removed from his building and that was the last they ever heard of him. For those lucky Lonely Guys whose fever did break, it was full recovery until the time rolled around for them to get sick again. In the New Sickness, fever breaks almost automatically, bringing the Lonely Guy to the door of health. Unhappily, he rarely makes it through. Responsibility lies squarely at the feet of the New Drugs which are game enough in taking on disease but lack the killer instinct. As a result, a small cadre of germs invariably survives, winded, but dead game and ready to sail back in when conditions are favorable.

In the New Sickness, fewer people drop dead— but everyone is a little bit sick all year round.

Going with Your Sickness

At the first sign of illness, many Lonely Guys quickly take on excellent habits, wearing sweaters, avoiding drafts, washing their vegetables before they eat them. Some sign on at gyms, while others fly south to "bake out." Once a germ takes hold, however, it is too late for admirable behavior. All the sit-ups in the world won't cure bronchitis. No one ever "baked out" the flu. The effort that goes into a last-minute try for health may bring on An Extra Sickness, which you don't need.

A sensible plan is to lie back and Go with Your Sickness; try to understand it and get as much out of it as possible.

Dealing with Doctors

Each year, testimonial dinners are held for crusty old doctors who braved the elements, year after year, to visit sick patients. Rare is the word spoken in praise of those valiant sick fellows, many of them dead, who braved the elements to visit doctors who would not come to see them.

Unless you live in a stubborn little community in Northern Minnesota, where people give to the land and the land gives back to them, it is unrealistic to expect your doctor to visit you when you're sick. He'll claim that he is too busy. The truth is he doesn't want to. Why should he fight traffic just to see another desperately ill person. You've seen one, you've seen them all.

Unless you can prove legally that your vital functions are slipping away—howls of agony won't do—you will have to settle for a phone diagnosis. The most important thing for the doctor to know is what color your phlegm is now—so make sure you have this information in advance. Unless it is an offbeat shade, like sienna, this should tip him off to the nature of your disease. If it is swamp green, don't bother to tell him since it is probably too late to do anything about it, and there is no point in upsetting him. Those who live in large impersonal high-rises—and are not sure of the color—can take a little down to the doorman who in most cases will be happy to check it out.

In a phone diagnosis, it is not important that the doctor grab on to the exact disease you have. The main idea is for him to prescribe a medicine that will give you enough energy to get to his office—so that he does not have to go to your place.

A Further Note on Doctors. Many Lonely Guys are more afraid of their doctors than they are of sickness. Rather than call up and get yelled at, they would rather quietly pack it in. Ask yourself this question: Do I have to psyche myself up to call the doctor, as if he were Jacqueline Onassis? If you do, you've got the wrong man.

Avoid funny doctors and those with a colorful mode of expressing themselves.

Here are some lines you don't need to hear from a doctor:

- You'd better sit down for this one.
- What do you have? Oh, I don't know, what would you like?
- I saw your stomach X rays. Looks like a goddamned junkyard in there.

Temperature as a Friend

Many Lonely Guys have a Fear of Temperature. Leave it to them, and they would choose not to have any at all, which is absurd, since everyone needs some. Far from being an enemy, temperature can be a friend, a sharp-eyed scout, warning of unattractive rapids up ahead. Admittedly, temperature can get out of control, going over to the other side. In such cases, it should be fought with every means available, like the Fourth Reich.

A high temperature is not always the result of illness. Sometimes, it's brought on by wearing too many sweaters. Or too much time in a sauna. Many a Lonely Guy will be shocked to see that his temperature is 109, theoretically taking him out of the battle.

A possibility is that he has forgotten to "shake down" the thermometer, the most important thing in temperature. This procedure calls for nimble wrists and great energy, none of which the Lonely Guy has when he is sick. Only small NBA forwards can really shake down a thermometer properly.

Reading a thermometer is mostly luck. There is a split second when the mercury lines up with the proper digit, but unless the sick Lonely Guy is on constant alert, like a radar man in the Aleutians, he will miss it and that will be it for the day. In theory, it should be simple to design a thermometer that says "Your temperature is 102" and throws in your horoscope as well, like a drugstore scale. For reasons known only to them, the powerful thermometer bloc has decided against this.

Lonely Guy Chicken Soup

For years, the chicken has been maligned as an absurd and
ridiculous-looking creature. Despite these scurrilous attacks,
the chicken good-naturedly continues to sacrifice himself in
order to provide mankind with the healthiest of all sick
foods—chicken soup. No longer do Jewish women hold the
monopoly on its preparation. The gentile woman who is not
in too much of a hurry because of her budding career can
make a perfectly respectable variety.

If he can muster the strength to crawl* into the kitchen
and lift a chicken into a pot, the sick Lonely Guy can make
a decent chicken soup of his own. All he need do is surround
the chicken with soup greens, adding a beef bone of the kind
that is normally tossed to Golden Retrievers if he wishes.
The pot should be filled with water so that it covers the
chicken and the chicken cannot see out over it. Salt should
be used sparingly. There is plenty of time for overkill later.

Lonely Guy Chicken Soup should never be rushed. Eating soup with a raw chicken sitting in it can set you back
irreversibly. On the other hand, do not let it cook until you
are already fully recovered and don't need it. A particular
problem for the sick Lonely Guy is having to get out of bed
every few minutes to skim off the fat. A way around that is
to leave it on. This is not to suggest that you eat the soup
with the fat on it. That *would* delay your cure. The idea is to
let the fat sit there until the soup appears to be cooked; then
put the chicken on a plate, and slide the soup into the freezer.
(Make sure you are wearing warm clothes during this part
of the operation, a ski outfit, ideally.) The fat will congeal
into a thick lid, something along the lines of a manhole
cover. After half an hour, unless the sick Lonely Guy is at

---

*Don't be ashamed to crawl when you're sick. It is not as if you've
been brought to your knees by tyranny.

death's door, he should be strong enough to lift, or at least
roll, the lid off the soup.

Sick Reading

Sick reading should be on the bland side. Generally speaking, it is a good idea to avoid Greek tragedy, Aeschylus being
the worst of all writers for the bedridden Lonely Guy. The
adventures of Prometheus, bound to a rock, or hundred-
headed Typhoeus, trying to get back at Zeus for burying him
in the slime, are not a pathway to brighter spirits. The same
is true of works on Industrial Safety in the Po Valley. Stick
to simple, wondrous stories. Fairy tales and pirate yarns are
ideal, although you may experience a shiver of regret that
you are no longer a prepubescent Lonely Guy.

Benefits of the New Sickness

Many sick Lonely Guys assume that the second they take
one step out of bed they have to forfeit all sick privileges.
This is not true. In preparing for a sickness, the Lonely Guy
with foresight will gather round him—or at least have
within crawling distance—all the sick stuff he'll need: cough
drops, orange juice, Kleenex, something to throw the old
Kleenex in. But once he's an officially sick fellow and sees
he's forgotten something, that doesn't mean he has to do
without it.

In the New Sickness, you can get out of bed and actually
sit on a couch and still be considered a sick fellow. Even if
you were to slip into a pair of French slacks and take a walk
in the hall, technically speaking, you would still be a sick
guy. It isn't being in bed—or your outfit—that determines
sick status. It's how lousy you feel. So long as you don't go
speeding down the Pacific Coast Highway in an open car,
you're covered.

Sick Air

The sick Lonely Guy needs fresh air but at the same time must avoid drafts, which are instant killers. A way to achieve this goal is to open the window, letting the fresh air in, and at the same time deflecting it with some kind of shield, a punk rock poster, for example. Window air is healthful, but tends to be chilly. Keep the radiator on full, but bear in mind the dangers of an entirely separate illness—Radiator Fever. A way to fend this off is to use a room humidifier which will moisten the dry radiator heat. The danger here is that the humidifier, unless carefully controlled, will turn the air dank and fetid, like unexplored sections of the Amazon. Getting sick air just right requires tremendous energy. The Lonely Guy might be better off just lying there and hoping for the best—or exploring some means of bringing in packages of air.

Après-Flu

A moment will come when the Lonely Guy has been in bed long enough and is ready to leave his sickness behind. Whatever charm the sickness had for him has disappeared. He's taken the last tetracycline pill in his five-day series. Theoretically, he should be ready to plunge back into the drabness of his life. Except that he is still sick. Patience is required at this juncture. There is no point in getting angry and trying to sue somebody. Germs very often are tied to a schedule of their own which does not conform to that of the Lonely Guy. It may be a simple matter of their wanting to stick around a bit longer, like getting in an extra day of skiing at Aspen.

When your sickness is at an end, don't make the mistake of telling everyone about it. The Lonely Guy who announces he's been running 102 degrees all week should not be surprised when pretty girls fail to throw their arms around him.

The details of an illness are simply not that fascinating. Few people will be enraptured by stories about postnasal drip. It isn't as if you've spent a month in Gabon, among the Abongo.

The sick Lonely Guy is often convinced that his business affairs have come to a grinding halt. This makes it difficult for him to lie back and get the maximum benefit from his illness. Once he's recovered, he may find that things ran quite smoothly. Vouchers got signed. Despite his absence at the helm, *Yogurt Magazine* shipped right on schedule. The mature Lonely Guy will not be dismayed by this news. On the contrary, it will sharpen his perspective, confirming his suspicion that his efforts in life follow a certain pattern.

Illness offers the Lonely Guy a chance to strike out in a new direction. Too enfeebled to shave, he will be in an excellent position to try out a new beard. His inability to keep down food will get him off to a running start on a new diet. Illness will give him the chance to lie back and get out of the race, in which he was lagging anyway. Most of all, it will offer him a chance to settle, once and for all, the question that nags at all Lonely Guys—considering the quality of his life, is he better off up and around, or in bed with a numbing fever?

Business Affairs

One summer, he worked as a busboy in a hotel. An obnoxious woman kept him coming and going round the clock. She insisted on extra portions and immaculate service. At the end of the summer, she gave him a pair of one-dollar bills for his trouble. In the style of a young Dominguín, he tossed the money back at her and walked away. But he could not resist looking over his shoulder. He saw her pick up the money and put it in her purse, thoroughly delighted to have it back.

    As a Lonely Guy, you probably find the business world sinister and mysterious and wish it would all go away. Having let yourself slide a bit, you are probably willing to let your financial affairs go further down the drain as well. *Don't do that.* Loneliness is expensive. It takes a lot of money to keep it going. You need throw pillows. You've got to have cookies, liverwurst sandwiches. You have to have a TV set to lull you to sleep. What about your eardrops bill, your bathrobes and your cotton balls?

    Whether or not you have the strength for it, you have to enter the Dollar War. As a Lonely Guy, you are in a unique position to do so, since what else do you have to do?

    Only by running a tight financial ship can you be lonely with confidence and security.

    What follows is a guide to the tricky ins and outs of Lonely Guy Financial Affairs.

Loans

Getting Money from a Friend. Banks, by tradition, never lend money to people who need it. On the other hand, they are delighted to hand over vast sums to people who haven't the slightest use for it. So normally, you will have to borrow money from a friend. In this type of loan, your only obligation is to call up now and then and explain why you haven't paid it back. If the friend calls *you,* he is being rude. Threaten never to borrow money from him again. (There is no need to follow through on your threat.)

Always ask for twice as much money as you need since even a close friend will automatically cut your request in half. Once in a while you may hit the jackpot and get exactly what you have asked for.

Remember, the friend who loaned you the money has done A Good Thing for you. There is no need to run up to him in a restaurant and throw a drink in his face. Many Lonely Guys get confused on this point. It's not the friend's fault that you needed money and he was generous enough to give it to you. (Although it *is* true he could have gotten it over there a little faster. And shouldn't he have *sensed* that you were broke? He's supposed to be a friend, isn't he?)

Getting Money from a Poor Guy. Another good person to borrow money from is a Poor Guy, a starving relative, ideally. Being a needy fellow, he's learned to squeeze every dime and as a result he has socked away plenty in his day. And don't feel bad about borrowing from him, even though he is starving. You're giving him a chance to feel important, possibly for the first time in his life, and that's not mashed potatoes.

Getting Money Back from a Woman. Be cautious about lending money to a woman. Women are equal in almost every way but lag behind seriously when it comes to paying back money. If you ask to have it back, you'll be called a sexist and, almost as bad, an insensitive swine. So when you lend money to a woman, write it off immediately and hope you get it back some day in That Other Department.

Paying Back Loans. One theory holds that when you borrow money, you should pay it back a little at a time. In short, give your creditor something to let him know you are thinking of him. In the words of a famous New York bookie, "Make sure you don't avoit my eyes." This makes sense so long as you pick the right figure. If you've borrowed $10,000, don't send off a check for $18.50, which will only serve as an irritant.

And it's generally not a good idea to send over something other than money—produce, for example, or a sweater. Stick to money. A bag of string beans, however well-meant, will only antagonize your creditor.

Second Loans. Having borrowed money from one person, you'll probably scout around and try to find someone else to borrow from. This is ridiculous. You're much better off going back to the first fellow. He's the one who gave you the money in the first place. That proved he had some. And by this time, he's had time to save up some more. The first guy is your man.

Credit Cards

Getting a Credit Card. If you're a Lonely Guy with a steady job, you should have no trouble getting a credit card. On the other hand, Lonely Guy Nobel Prize Laureates may be in for some rough sledding. The reasoning of the credit card companies is that just because someone's won a Nobel Prize, it doesn't mean he is going to win another one. There is no consistency to it. So why should they take a risk on a person like that? In other words, if you're Saul Bellow and

stubbornly refuse to take a job in venetian blinds, you can
forget about credit cards.

Using Your Credit Card. The most important thing to
find out about a credit card is how long they give you before
they run over and grab it back. It's important to have several
cards so you can mix up your punches, so to speak. When
Diner's Club decides it's time to come after you, you can stop
using it and begin to take advantage of American Express.

Pay no attention to stores and restaurants that say they
honor credit cards. Even if they worship and obey them and
throw garlands of roses at their feet, it doesn't do you any
good unless they actually *accept* them.

Hookers can be charged to your credit cards, but must be
billed through organic honey companies. Remember, your
accountant will sternly demand to know why you are spending $6000 a year on organic honey, so develop a little thing
for it.

Losing Your Credit Card. A big fear is that you will lose
your credit card and the finder will immediately run over
and charge a cabin cruiser to your name. This is an unnec-
essary worry. When the cabin cruiser salesman sees *your* name
on the card, he will know it is all a big joke.

Disposing of Your Credit Card. At the end of the year,
be careful when you are tearing up your credit card. One of
the most insidious wounds you can get is from the edge of
an invalidated BankAmericard.

Banks

The Right Bank for You. The Right Bank for You is
one that is far away. If it's too close, you'll be running over
there all the time; one way or another you won't have any
money left. Also, the closer the bank, the easier it is for it to

get at you. Try to come up with a bank that uses phones. When you are in financial hot water, many of them will say, "This guy is fading fast. All we have to do is apply a little pressure and we can bring him to his knees."

A friendly bank will call and tell you when you're over-drawn instead of crushing you by keeping it a secret. This will not really change the situation. It isn't as if you'll be able to run over there with a bale of money. But at least you'll be prepared for what's in store for you.

Banking by Mail. Never bank by mail. The tension involved in waiting to see if your money ever got there is one of the big contributors to cardiac trouble in America. Even if your name is Wodjikaciwizc, the bank will find *another* Wodjikaciwizc and return your bankbook to him.

Bank Etiquette. When you're standing in line at the bank, try to avoid peeking at the other person's deposit slip, to see if he's putting in more than you.

Bouncing Checks. Once checks start bouncing, there is almost no way to get them to stop, i.e., when the first one bounces, you can be sure that others will follow. The smart-est thing is to get out of town for a while. Go to the Hamptons or Malibu for the weekend. When you get back, you'll feel more relaxed and better able to go over to the bank and start piecing through the rubble.

Money Savers

A Subscription to *Mitten*. The quickest way for you to start saving is to cut down on the number of dirty maga-zines you buy. You should be able to get through on thirty a month. Try to zero in on your area of interest. If you're mainly interested in pictures of women wearing mittens, face up to it and stop kidding yourself. Take out a subscription to *Mitten* and hold it right there. Don't squander your money on magazines featuring nonmitten pictures.

Lonely Guys of the Future. Another surefire money saver is to put all your loose change in a bottle and set it aside for a favorite nephew who is away at school. When he comes home for the holidays, *don't give him the money.* Keep it yourself. If you're too sweet a guy to go through with this, skim off the quarters and give him what's left. This same technique can be applied to trust funds for kids, those Lonely Guys of the Future, redeemable when they hit age twenty-one. Before that happens, start siphoning off the money, ostensibly for the kids' care, but actually to pay off the huge credit card bills you must face up to.

Bargain Hunting. Learn to think economically and to hunt for bargains. When veal is sky-high, pork butts may be dirt cheap. By eating pork butts every day for a couple of months, you can save a small fortune.

And don't forget off-season buying. The time to buy a heavy winter coat is not during the winter when you need it, but on the most sweltering day of the year when you can snap one up for a song. But be careful. Try it on quickly, and then whip it off quickly so you avoid heat prostration.

Things are always cheaper in some neighborhoods than in others. But don't buy any old thing just because it's cheap. What good will a hat rack do you, if you've left your hat in Toronto? Even if it is cheap. The Lonely Guy who lugs home a giant bale of radishes often forgets that he will have to eat his way through them in order to justify this.

Insurance

By all means, take out insurance. Everyone has to do his bit to keep up this huge, wonderful industry that employs so many fine Americans. But never assume that you're actually going to collect on an insurance claim. The companies *say* they've paid off claims, but can you name a single fellow who has, as an example, lost all his suits and gotten paid back for them? Generally, the only ones who ever collect on insurance are drought victims.

An absolute must for the Lonely Guy is glove insurance. As a Lonely Guy, you probably lose around a half-dozen pairs a year, especially if you live in a chilly climate. Insurance companies, usually tough customers, are fairly softhearted when it comes to settling glove claims.

Safe Deposit Boxes

The One Big Danger. It's perfectly all right for you to sign up for a safe deposit box so long as you are aware of The One Big Danger. As the years roll along, you'll start imagining you've left all kinds of valuable items in there. This will set you up for a serious disappointment when you open it up and all you find is a skate key and some *Saturday Evening Posts*. Even worse, there may be some old sandwiches in there that you forgot about. So keep a safe deposit box, but don't start fooling yourself about what you've left in it.

Not Losing the Key. Make sure to keep the key in a safe place. Otherwise, the box will have to be blasted open. This costs more than you make on six months of unemployment.

Taxes

Fear of the Tax Man. Don't be afraid of the tax collector who, after all, is just a human being with the same doubts and inner fears that all of us have. Try to avoid direct contact with him, though, since if you meet face to face he will tend to know that you are lying through your teeth.

Get your accountant to tell the tax man that you are having a bit of a nervous disorder, which will always be more or less true.

If the tax man insists on seeing you in person, remember that the only way to deal with the government is to hurl a lot of paper at them. Fill a laundry bag with tickets, coupons, old *Playbills* from Broadway shows, veal piccata recipes, anything . . . dump it on the tax collector's desk and say: "It's all in there, fella."

Also, try to establish some common ground with the tax collector. Not something ridiculous. It's not important whether you both saw Ethel Merman in the original *Gypsy*. But maybe you both went to the same archery camp. Finding this out may not give you a tax advantage, but at least you will have come up with a talking point.

Lawyers and Accountants

Selecting a Lawyer. One of the secrets of business is to hire people who are good at it. This means taking on a crackerjack lawyer. Don't sign up with a huge law firm that has many partners and important clients such as the state of Oklahoma. Each time you visit your lawyer, he'll make you feel as though you're muscling in on Oklahoma's time. You are better off with a small scrappy guy who will yell and holler at people on your behalf, while you stay in the background being your charming self.

Paying the Lawyer. It's important to remember that lawyers charge for their time. So make sure you're calling about something important. Don't phone him to find out who he likes more, De Niro or Pacino. Or because you're a little lonely. Make sure that you're at least calling to sue somebody. And no matter what the lawyer says, be sure to go ahead and sue because you're already deeply in debt to the lawyer as a result of calling him.

Selecting an Accountant. Most accountants will get infuriated when you eat in restaurants. They are pale fellows who don't have any fun and don't want you to have any either. They want you to live in one room and eat boiled potatoes. Get an accountant who doesn't mind if you eat out once in a while. Make sure your accountant is not afraid of the government. You don't need one who calls and says: "Jesus, they really got us now. I don't see how we're gonna squirm out of this one."

A good accountant will also lend you a couple of bucks when you're in a jam.

Stationery

Don't throw your money away on expensive stationery. Just rip off the ends of things, bread wrappers, telephone bills, other guys' letters, and use that. This will beef up your image as a modest Carl Sandburg–type of fellow. Here is a sample of some perfectly acceptable Lonely Guy Stationery:

Credit Ratings

Once you get a bad credit rating, it will follow you all your life and get passed on to your children, like hemophilia. The most amazing law on record says that credit companies are allowed to keep sending out bad reports on you for seven

years after you've made your record spotless. If the credit
companies had to keep their records up to date, it would
require a lot of time and effort and get them all upset. No
one wants to see this. So Congress passed this law to keep
the credit companies from becoming cranky.

Only guys named Chip who live in Darien, Connecticut,
have good credit ratings.

An Ace in the Hole

A Special Invitation. If you are under attack from a collection agent, you may have an Ace in the Hole you didn't
know about. Instead of barricading your doors and hiding
under the bed, invite the collection agent in to see your apartment. No agent in the world, no matter how hard-hearted,
will be able to stand up to the sight of a Lonely Guy Apartment. A typical reaction will be: "Jesus, no one can live like
this. I'm sorry I ever bothered you." The agent will then
burst into tears and go away.

The Across-the-River Dodge

If you live in a high tax state, you can save a fortune by
taking a small apartment across the river in a neighboring state
where the taxes are lower. But you've actually got to live in
that apartment. Dropping in once in a while to watch a little
daytime TV will not appease the government. There are special teams of tax guys who run across-the-river bed checks and
won't give you a tax credit unless they see that your head
touches the pillow every night and that you're fast asleep.

Wills

Should You Make One Out. Lonely Guys often assume
that making out a will is the same as dropping dead. This is
absurd. It's just preparation.

Keeping It Up to Date. Many Lonely Guys have dropped dead only to find they have accidentally left their money to the one who threw them out. So keep your will up to date. Find a Loved One, any old Loved One, and leave your money to that person.

The loneliest development in the world is when a Lonely Guy leaves his money to a highway.

Where to Do It. There is no reason for you to make out your will in a gloomy atmosphere. It doesn't have to be done in a crypt, with your attorney acting as Boris Karloff. The best place to draw up a will is in a cocktail lounge.

Investments

Real Estate. The soundest investment continues to be real estate, which always goes up, until the time you want to sell it, at which point the market is generally "a little soft." The trick is to get rid of your real estate when you don't want to, when wild horses couldn't get you to part with it.

Never buy property in a country in which there is even a single insurgent up in the hills. Soon, mercenaries from Katanga will join him and they will all come down and get your land.

Dwarf Loopholes and Broadway. In the Sixties, many people got tremendous tax advantages by investing in dwarf ponies, but that loophole has now been plugged up. So have the dwarf date tree and dwarf turkey loopholes. All that dwarf stuff has been plugged up.

Under no circumstance should the Lonely Guy be talked into investing in or supporting the Arts. Even giving comfort to them is highly speculative. Unless he gets a crack at a hot Velázquez. Don't be talked into backing a Broadway show with the promise that you will get to sleep with the leading lady. One of the cardinal rules of show business is that the leading lady belongs to the director. If he insists, the investor will be allowed to watch the director sleep with her.

Stock Tips. The stock market is tricky. Many Lonely Guys bought stocks in the late Sixties on the assumption that the entire country, from Maine to Los Angeles, was going to be at leisure, every man and woman in the U.S. just bowling away the day. This never happened. Everyone is working harder than ever. If you had invested in work stuff—lightbulbs, desks, coffeebreak wagons—you would be on easy street.

The best stock tips come from waiters in exclusive restaurants who get to overhear this kind of information while scraping up the bread crumbs of important customers.

Try to sneak in and see movies before they open officially. If you really love the movie, and think it's going to be a blockbuster, run out and purchase the stock of the movie studio that made it. But make sure you're not the only one in the audience that loves it. If it's about giant man-eating boll weevils, and everyone else is snoring, you may be the only weevil man out there.

Hidden Resource

Even though your back seems to be to the wall, you may not be as broke as you think. And no one is talking here about the potassium in your body after you keel over. Forget that. The phone company, for example, is probably holding a $25 deposit that technically belongs to you. You may own a life insurance policy that's worth another fifty bucks in cash. Throw in deposit bottles, Canadian coins you never bothered to cash in, Vegas casino chips, and little folded-up fives and tens in old windbreakers. It starts to add up.

The average Lonely Guy is worth around $185 more than he thinks he is.

Retirement Plans

As a Lonely Guy, you've been more or less retired all along.
When it comes time for you to pack it in, how are you going
to know? A more positive way to look at it is that a Retirement Plan is more essential to the Lonely Guy than to the
everyday fellow. Most people are a little tired when they
retire. Not the Lonely Guy. You've been saving up energy.
When you hit sixty-five you really want to cut loose. So you
should have a sound Retirement Plan, one that gives you as
much cash as possible to throw around.

Lonely Guys, if they make it, are among the peppiest of
old guys.

Sum-up

While you sleep, an army of tax men, lawyers, accountants, agents and other assorted bad guys are out to get what
little you have. If it's $1000, they not only want every dime
of it, but they want a strict accounting of how you're going
to get up the next $1000.

You can't win that war. No one can. In that sense, every
American is just another Lonely Guy.

It will take all of your energies just to break even.

But you must not just keel over. Never simply hand over
your money. At least do a lot of pissing and moaning and
then hand it over. Let the sonsofbitches know they've been
in a fight.

You may be an American Lonely Guy, *but you're also a man.*

Hats off to you and yours in your worthwhile struggle to
become a financially solvent Lonely Guy.

On the Couch

As a child, he had a lovely singing voice but was quite shy about using it. He would consent to sing for company, but only if he could be under the piano. His sister would accompany him, and only when the song was completed would he come out from beneath the piano to take his bow.

At college, he agreed to be the M.C. for a variety show. Several hundred young women were in attendance, crossing and uncrossing their legs. He told a few jokes and then the microphone went dead and he could not silence the crowd. He fainted, and a hated economics major took over for him. When he was brought around, a fellow named Schapiro said: "I heard your jokes. They were terrific. What'd you have to faint for?"

He studied history under a professor who took the position that the Germans were not solely responsible for the start of World War One. One day, he was chosen to debate this subject with some visiting students from Cambridge. They smoked pipes, wore shawls and seemed quite scholarly. He began with the statement: "The Germans were not solely responsible for the start of World War One."

"Indeed," said one of the Englishmen. "Why not?"

Suddenly, he forgot all the critical dates and codicils and Serbo-Croatian treaties he needed to support his argument. He was afraid of the fellow's shawl.

"Because they just weren't," he said and fainted.

When he recovered, he was told that a teammate had taken over and held the Englishmen to a tie, but that did not make him feel any better.

Can a psychiatrist help the Lonely Guy?

No reputable one will take him dancing or snuggle up to him on cold winter nights. But this option can give him something tangible to look forward to several times a week —a visit to the psychiatrist's office.

Many Lonely Guys have been frightened off by the public behavior of psychiatrists. Famed ones vomit routinely at dinner parties, pinching at hostesses and wrestling them to the ground. Others lose control of their sphincters at bond rallies and have to be led off in diapered disgrace. In spite of these shortcomings, a psychiatrist *can* be of aid to the Lonely Guy. One need only cite the example of Walter Alston, a hopelessly inept ballplayer who nonetheless coached the Brooklyn and Los Angeles Dodgers to immortality.

The decision to tie on with a psychiatrist should not be approached casually, the way one might stroll into a supermarket to check the new mustards. Psychiatry is only for those in urgent need of it. The best candidate for treatment may be the Lonely Guy who has no choice in the matter and is dragged in, feet first, foaming over with neuroses.

Choosing the Right Man

Great care should be taken in the selection of a psychiatrist since both doctor and patient are in for a long haul. Treatment often drags on endlessly, until one of the participants falls by the wayside. If it is the psychiatrist, his wife may very well seize the reins and see the treatment through in the tradition of stalwart congressional widows. Should the Lonely Guy be the first to fall, his sons may want to leap onto the couch and wrap up their dad's complexes.

The Lonely Guy should take care to interview several doctors and not snap up the first to take an interest in him, as if he were at a Singles' Bar. One method of picking a psychiatrist is to think of someone who once behaved disgracefully—running up to strangers and head-butting them to the ground—and no longer does. The chances are that such a fellow has been taken in hand by a good psychiatrist. He may even *be* a good psychiatrist.

Though any old doctor can be of some help to the Lonely Guy, there is no reason to test this theory by signing on with a fellow who wears offensive suits or uses a whorish cologne. Obvious mismatches are to be avoided. The tall and shambling Lonely Guy will not flourish under the care of a short aggressive fellow who kicks at his shins to get his attention. Ultimately, the Lonely Guy must choose a psychiatrist whose style and manner he admires. No further thought should be given to the rejected ones, most of whom will recover in several months; worrying will not help them.

The Bargain

A first meeting should be frank, with possible sticking points dissolved openly. Let's say the psychiatrist is an ex-Nazi. Rather than have this fact crop up later at some delicate point in the treatment—it should be put right out on the table. The ex-Nazi Lonely Guy should be equally forthright about his background.

The delicate matter of the doctor's fee is bound to come up at any first meeting. Some Lonely Guys, new to the couch, will be shocked and personally offended to learn that the doctor charges any fee at all, seeing this as one more example of moral decay in America. The fair-minded Lonely Guy, on the other hand, will agree that the psychiatrist has just as much right to loll about on Caribbean beaches as the next fellow.

The standard fee for treatment is in the neighborhood of $40–60 per fifty-minute hour. (The ten minutes between patients is designed to give the psychiatrist a chance to catch

his breath, make a few calls and perhaps slap on a deodorant.) The Lonely Guy should beware of the doctor who
charges some offbeat fee such as $37.50 per half hour. Also
suspect is the fellow who offers summer discounts and
earlybird specials. On occasion, psychiatrists have been
known to trim off a few dollars for the demonstrably needy
patient. The Lonely Guy who benefits from a reduced fee
should refrain from strutting about the waiting room and
lording it over the other patients.

How to Behave in the Office

Since the doctor will be watching him like a hawk, the
Lonely Guy must be careful of his behavior in the psychiatrist's office where the most casual gesture takes on great
significance. The Lonely Guy who kicks his feet up on the
doctor's desk may be expressing some coquettish need to
titillate the doctor with a cancan. A soft burp in the palm
of the hand, innocuous in the workaday world, may represent an all-out attack on the doctor's values. The Lonely Guy
who uses the psychiatrist's john in mid-session is taking his
life in his hands. A single visit will lead to endless specula-
tions about toilet training, especially if the doctor is from
Vienna where great stock is placed in such matters.

A wise course for the Lonely Guy is to do as little as
possible.

Early on, the Lonely Guy will have to decide just how much
he wants to tell the doctor. There is no need, for example, to
bring up the subject of his mom; he has a right to some pri-
vacy, after all. The same is true of sex; surely there is enough
trouble in this world without getting down in the gutter. As
a general rule, the Lonely Guy who tells the doctor too much
risks losing his mystery and allure. No longer under his spell,
the psychiatrist may turn his attention to other patients.

Theoretically, there is no boundary to what the patient
can tell the psychiatrist, who is fond of saying that he is not

a moral censor. Whether it be masturbatory practices on dogsleds or overinvolvement with kneesox, the doctor has seen and heard it all. A word of caution, however. Even the most worldly-wise psychiatrist has his limits. The Lonely Guy who rambles on endlessly about his erotic interest in slime mold may eventually be shown to the door.

Couch Strategies

Normally, the psychiatrist will insist that the Lonely Guy lie down on the fabled couch. This is so that the doctor's presence does not become an interference, the Lonely Guy getting caught up in a distracting fantasy about his wrist hairs. There are several advantages to the use of the couch. Should the memory of a dead uncle cause the Lonely Guy to burst into tears, the psychiatrist—unless he rudely peers over— will not be able to witness this spectacle. Then, too, the couch can serve as a litmus paper of mental health. The Lonely Guy who clings to it and has to be pulled off at the end of sessions quite clearly has some distance to go in his cure. Conversely, the Lonely Guy who suddenly vaults off and refuses to spend another minute on it may be knocking at the door of self-confidence.

A disadvantage to the use of the couch is that it leaves the doctor unattended. There is no telling what he's up to back there. To rectify this situation, the nimble Lonely Guy, using the crook of his arm as a periscope, will be able to peer back and monitor his activities. Another technique is to catch the doctor's reflection in a shoe mirror.

As a general rule, no psychiatrist should be left unwatched for more than ten minutes at a time.

Most psychiatrists' couches will have lingering traces of perfume left by attractive young women who turned up for early sessions. There is no point in the Lonely Guy being shy about his interest in these. Quite boldly, he should ask the psychiatrist if it's all right to sniff some in.

How It All Works

The basic style of the treatment is for the Lonely Guy to toss off story after aimless story until he stumbles across something of value. It is a great time-waster for the Lonely Guy to use up his fifty minutes on matters that are important to him, since they are never at the root of his difficulty. Only items that are preposterously insignificant are of the slightest bit of therapeutic use—he may as well get on with it and talk about them.

Under the psychiatrist's gentle guidance, the Lonely Guy will be steered toward a breakthrough—that is, a shaft of insight in which he sees that someone he always considered a loved one is a swine. Or that some swine is a loved one. The Lonely Guy himself may turn out to be a swine. Having arrived at this point, the Lonely Guy should be cautioned against leaping off the couch and organizing congratulatory benefits in his name. He should realize he's at about the same stage as the French who first broke ground on the Panama Canal. Only decades later did the first ship go sliding through.

If the Lonely Guy is unable to produce a breakthrough, the psychiatrist may show up one morning in a tutu, or posing as a Hartz Mountain transvestite, tapping at the underside of a breast and winking lasciviously at his patient. The Lonely Guy should see this tableau for what it is—a kind of psychiatric playacting designed to jiggle forth the breakthrough from the repressed Lonely Guy. Only then should he decide if he wants to join the doctor beneath the couch.

The Importance of Dreaming

Psychiatrists routinely use dreams as a centerpiece of treatment. Many Lonely Guys are under the impression that their dreams are brought in nightly from the West Coast, packaged by the same people who created "Roller Girls." When

one is flimsy in plot, or an out-and-out turkey, their impulse
is to call the coast and raise hell, like a cable TV subscriber.

In reality, the Lonely Guy himself is the author of his
dreams, responsible for gaps in story line, lapses in taste and
even dreadful acting. Not only does he write and direct his
dreams, he also plays all the parts in them. If he dreams he is
a seaman, adrift on the high seas with an ill-mannered Kurd,
he is not only the seaman but the Kurd as well. There is only
one exception to this rule: the horrifying dream in which the
Lonely Guy is being chased by a sinister man. Examined
closely, this awful fellow can be seen to be not the Lonely Guy
but the psychiatrist, perhaps trying to collect his fees.

Dreams are essential to treatment and most therapists will
insist that you have them. The Lonely Guy who has trouble
in this area will be encouraged to eat chili peppers before
turning in for the night.

False Mental Health

After a few sessions, the Lonely Guy will feel he is brimming over with mental health and may be tempted to dash
through the streets with great goat cries of stability. This is
a misleading time, similar to the "phony peace" that spread
through Europe when Hitler conquered Poland and stopped
momentarily to catch his breath. The psychiatrist has simply given the Lonely Guy a taste, a swatch, if you will, of
well-being, of normalcy. The Lonely Guy may rest assured
that in no time at all he will be plunged back into the gloom
he has come to know and love, and that he will still need
the psychiatrist.

Who Is *That Owlish Fellow, Anyway?*

Ultimately, the Lonely Guy will wind up spending more
time with the psychiatrist than he did with his mom. It is
only natural for him to become curious about the fellow.

What summer camp did he go to? Who are his friends? Is his wife a charmer? When asked about his personal life, the psychiatrist, depending upon his discipline, will either shrug or smile thinly.

The Unappeased Lonely Guy who spies on his doctor at night—or hires private eyes to follow him about—is in for a disappointment. For a psychiatrist, filling out a *Reader's Digest* sweepstakes blank is the height of rascality. Rare is the doctor who has been engaged to Liv Ullmann. On occasion, one will leap out of a high-rise, but most lead humdrum lives.

When It's Over

How can the Lonely Guy tell when his treatment is nearing the end? One theory is that it never quite does, and that Freud himself could have used a few brushup sessions. Certainly, there is no official ending, a giant production number bringing the curtain down on *My Fair Lady*. Often, the treatment simply winds down, both doctor and Lonely Guy admitting they can no longer stand the strain.

It might be some chance event that tells the story, a stranger setting fire to the Lonely Guy's gym shorts. Previously, this action would have offended the Lonely Guy and thrown him off his game. Thanks to his years on the couch, he will see that there is little to be done about it and simply swat down the flames, smile patiently at the twists and turns of fate, and go about his business.

Psychiatry cannot banish loneliness. But it can firm it up a bit—perhaps enable the Lonely Guy to see clearly and unflinchingly for the first time what he is and what he may always be—a you-know-what.

At the Typewriter

He wrote an essay in junior high school in which he used the phrase "Black clouds of Nazi oppression." The teacher took the position that no boy in junior high could make up such an expression. He was given a low grade and for the rest of the semester he was shunned as the boy who stole the phrase: "Black clouds of Nazi oppression."

As a Lonely Guy, you've got all that unhappiness and melancholy, just sitting there, going to waste. Why not cash in on it, using it for fun and profit? The way to do that is to become a writer.

You'll get to stare at people with blazing intensity and not be thought rude. You'll be able to sit alone over a drink, with bunched-up jaw muscles, as if life is too painful to contemplate; normally, this would be considered boring. Not if you're a writer.

If someone calls, and you don't feel like talking, all you have to say is "I'm working." The caller will retreat in embarrassment and shame, convinced he has caught you in mid-Canto and thrown off your rhythm. Your erratic behavior will be excused. If you are at a party and suddenly sling a model over one shoulder, slipping the Muenster cheese in your back pocket, someone will chuckle and say: "Don't mind him. He's one of those crazy writers."

You'll get to end love affairs abruptly, offering no explanation, and not be considered an ingrate. You're sensitive.
You have your work. Even your crushed and rejected girlfriend will fly to your defense.

How does all that sound to you, Lonely Guy?

If it's your kind of madness, read on.

What Kind of Writer Should I Be?

Absurdist. The easiest kind of writer to be is an absurdist.
All you've got to do is start jokes and not finish them. Have
a character ask: "Is that a Sloth sitting next to you?" and don't
let anyone answer. Let the question hang there, giving off
echoes of Alienation and the Spiritual Impoverishment of
Man. If you complete the joke, all you are is an amusing
fellow. No critic will take you seriously.

Satirist. A satirist is a fellow who writes with a cool and
veiled rage about the foibles of modern society. If you decide to be a satirist, make sure your rage is veiled. Calling
someone a "no-good sonofabitch" is not good satire.

It is difficult to support a family on satire.

Ironist. An ironist is a fellow who can't sustain a good
story. So he throws in a lot of stuff that doesn't fit. Twenty
pages, out of nowhere, on axle grease. Anyone who objects
to this long axle grease section has missed the irony.

It is impossible to support a family on irony.

Jewish-American Writer. All the fine Jewish writers insist that their writing is not Jewish. They are commenting
on the *human* condition, not the Jewish one. They can't help
it if it comes out sounding Jewish. This has created a need
for a new Jewish writer who admits that his material is a
little Jewish. Even if he is not Jewish.

What Should I Write About?

"**Mel was depressed.**" A lot of notable writing comes out of unhappiness. This does not mean you should hack off a toe just to make sure you're miserable. Go with what you have. As a Lonely Guy, you should be set up nicely in this area. Remember, though, that unalloyed misery on the page is not necessarily rousing.

The line "Mel was depressed" at the beginning of a book is no guarantee that the reader will fly through the pages to see if Mel ever gets to feel better. A few curiosity seekers, perhaps, but not enough to send the book zooming up the lists. At minimum, have Mel feel depressed as he is diving beneath a Sardinian reef, where no man has ever felt depressed before.

A Trip to Kabul. Does travel help? Not necessarily. You don't have to go to Kabul to write about it. In fact, some of the best Kabul stuff has been written by guys who never went near the place. All they did in preparation was to read a few books about the area, written by fellows who'd never been there either. What they all came up with was Mythic Kabul, something no local Kabul man could ever approximate. Kabul critics eat that up.

Nothing to Say. How can I write a book? you might ask. I've got nothing to say. Don't let that stop you. Very few writers have anything to say. The trick is to see how long you can conceal that from the reader. The most successful writers are ones who've been able to get away with it for the greatest number of pages and years.

Who Should I Write For?

This is an age-old dilemma. Who is that fellow whose face I should be staring at as I write? Who will laugh at my jokes?

If I write for someone smarter than I am, he'll see right through me. If I write for a dumb guy, I'll be writing a lot of dumb stuff. I can't write for myself. I'm on to all my old tricks. I'll put myself to sleep.

The best person to write for is Bianca Jagger.

Where Should I Begin My Story?

All new writers agonize over this question. Should I begin with Glynis contemplating the new maturity of her body? Or Andrew caught up in the aroma of fresh muffins? The answer is that it doesn't matter. If your destination is downtown Vancouver, the important thing is to get there. Any road will do.

It helps, however, to make your beginning relevant. Why make life difficult by kicking off a War of the Roses yarn with a list of your favorite movie stars. Unless you're one of those fellows who fiddles around with traditional concepts of time and space. Remember, though, that Twentieth isn't really interested in those fellows.

Tricks and Tools of the Trade

A Fascinating Typewriter. The kind of typewriter you choose will invariably influence your work. If you select a sturdy, high-backed type, you may find yourself taking on crusty, muckraking themes. Lashing out at the meat-packing industry and giving Lockheed a good tongue-lashing. A spare, cool-looking model that sends off a low impersonal hum will inevitably have you examining East-West themes, EuroComm and the complexities of modern industrial society. And you may not want to get into those areas.

So make sure you pick *your* kind of typewriter. And keep it fairly basic. The idea is to do fascinating work, not have a fascinating typewriter.

When You're Stuck. When you're stuck, switch over to a pencil. This will take you back to that time when you were a kid and writing was easy and natural and joyous. If this doesn't work, just be quiet when you're stuck and don't do anything for a while. Don't try to write your way out of it. No one wants to spend money for a book to see how the author tried to write his way out of something.

A Quiet Place. Do your writing in a quiet place. But not too quiet, or all you'll be able to write about is Alienation. This is not a good idea—unless Twentieth changes its mind and decides to get back into it.

Wide Margins. Use wide margins, not to cheat the publisher, but to give the reader a rest at the end of your sentences. A wide margin is like a pit stop to the weary reader.

Short or Long Sentences? Obviously, you've got to go with either short or long sentences. Short ones are good if you know what you're talking about. Otherwise, your ignorance will stand out. Long, run-on sentences were invented by writers who didn't know what they were getting at but figured they'd come up with something if they kept the sentence running on long enough, like the one you're reading.

Sights and Sounds and Smells. Try to re-create faithfully the sights and sounds and smells of everyday life. If you have trouble doing this, subtly smear a little marinara sauce at the bottom of the page.

Film Sales

Every writer dreams of selling his book to the movies. There is no shame in that. But no serious writer ever lets this influence his work. Or decides ahead of time that he is after a film sale. If it works out, fine. If not, no problem. So

the idea is to work on each sentence until you are satisfied
that it serves the best interests of twentieth-century literature. Only then should it be scanned thoroughly to see if
there is something for Redford in it.

The Female Point of View

Many great writers have never mastered the knack of
writing from the female point of view. Putting on a petti-
coat each time you come to the woman's part won't really
do it. And you'll be exhausted from changing clothes all the
time. The trick is to write the dialogue as if you are writing
it for a male:

"Shut up, you worthless swine," said Derek.

Then switch over and attribute this same line of dialogue
to a woman.

"Shut up, you worthless swine," said Susannah.

To cement the deal, you can do the following variation.

"Shut up, you worthless swine," said Susannah, prettily,
with a whispered rustle of her petticoats.

You are writing from the female point of view. And no
one will be able to guess your secret.

Sexy Writing

Any moron can write about surging breasts and tumescent loins. The trick is to be subtle about it, to keep the sex
out of view, but beating up against the surface. Make sure
it's beating up there, however. Don't write a page about
bread crumbs and expect the reader to get all turned on.

Critics

No serious writer pays the least bit of attention to critics.
He may stick his finger in one's eye every now and then. But
that's the extent of his interest.

Help from Other Writers

Other writers are the most generous of people when it comes to sharing their knowledge and craft. If you need encouragement, don't be shy about seeking out an established writer and asking him for help. The only time he'll clam up is when he senses you're about to get the picture.

The Hemingway Legacy

Few writers contributed more to literature than Ernest Hemingway. But he also caused a lot of damage. The worst thing he did was to announce that he did his best writing at "first light." Ever since then, writers have been rolling out of bed at four in the morning, cranky and irritable, pecking away. Did anyone ever catch Hemingway working then? He was a competitive fellow and may very well have been trying to get other writers to work when they were exhausted.

A Writer's Day

Here's the way to arrange your day as a writer. Forget "first light." Get up at a reasonable hour. It doesn't matter when— so long as you do get up. Eat a good breakfast, one that sticks to your ribs. As a writer, you need all the strength you can get. Read the newspapers and knock off around eleven or twelve magazines so that your work reflects the tenor of the times. Check the mail to see if anyone sent anything back. Smoke a cigar, which should get you a little drowsy. Drop off and get a little more sleep, since, as a writer, you need all the rest you can get.

When you wake up, eat a couple of nectarines to get your motor going again. Hunt and peck a few sentences. Call up a friend and try them out on him. If he doesn't fall on the floor laughing, throw them out. Check the mail again, in case you missed a letter that was wedged in the corner of the mailbox. Make up a few more sentences, but don't try them out on your friend this time. Go to the delicatessen, order a tongue sandwich and see if you can pick up anything from the interesting characters who work behind the counter. So your work reflects the tenor of delicatessen life.

On your way home, stop at the Chinese laundry, in case some of your shirts came back early. Be on the alert for interesting stuff to write about in the laundry. Way in the back, where they eat, and all the interesting family stuff goes on.

When you get back, see if the toaster needs cleaning. If so, go to work on it. It's hard to write when you know there's an accumulation of eleven months' worth of English muffin crumbs in there. While you're digging them out, you can be working up ahead, on your writing. Try a few more sentences. If all you can come up with are one or two, don't be discouraged. Remember, they add up. At the end of the year, you may have forty or fifty, which will put you ahead of Beckett. Call up some friends to make sure they're not getting anything done either.

Go out and pick up a fish for dinner. Make sure its eyes are sparkly. When you get back home, watch the six o'clock news, so that your work reflects the tenor of television. After dinner, hang out at a bar that's filled with colorful characters. If you hear something colorful, run home and write it down so you don't forget it. Only frequent nearby bars, so you're not exhausted from running back and forth. Don't pick up any girls. As a writer, you need all the energy you can store.

Before you go to bed, read some other guy's successful book and try to keep your anger in check.

There you are. A Day in the Life of a Writer. Not much different from yours, is it? Except that you'll be putting That Sinking Feeling to constructive use.

So what are you waiting for? Don't just sit there and ru-
minate. Hit those keys. Take a shot at fame, fortune, trips
to the Coast and an altogether new source of heartbreak and
misery.

Part Three

Perks

The Lonely Guy Wises Up

Finally, he saw what was wrong.

He was worrying too much about the wrong things.

He worried about Catfish Hunter's sore shoulder, Bill Walton's feet and whether Lyman Bostock could possibly play well enough to justify the 3.5 million the Angels had invested in him. He was still concerned about Willis Reed's knees. He worried about Sammy Davis' crushing schedule, Lorna Luft's apparent lack of a clear direction for her career and Cher's inability to find a meaningful relationship. McQueen's price concerned him and so did CBS's seeming inability to overtake pesky innovative ABC.

So one day he stopped worrying about these things and immediately he felt better.

All he had to do now was stop concerning himself with Carter's declining popularity and whether *Jaws 2* would outgross *Godfather I* and he would be in the clear.

The Lonely Guy
and His Dog

A dreadful fellow came to live in the neighborhood. He was blond, well-muscled, and although he pretended to be sixteen, the feeling was that he was secretly older, possibly in his twenties. He had a little white dog. He smashed younger boys against playground walls and hurled fully grown war veterans to the pavement. He seemed totally evil. The only thing that did not fit was the little white dog.

For the Lonely Guy who can't get along with a person, a dog may be just the ticket. He can start with a dog, see how it goes, and then shift over to a human being. Or he can stop with the dog. It's up to him.

But a dog has its limitations. Finally, it's only a dog. Just because it can run after a stick does not mean that it can field questions on Turkish politics. The Lonely Guy who yearns for a pretty and delightful young woman who works on a Drug Experimentation program at Barnard College will not be satisfied with a dog. One of the reasons a Lonely Guy will hug and squeeze his dog so much is that he is unconsciously trying to turn it into a witty person. This cannot be done. A dog must be put in perspective. Otherwise, the Lonely Guy will wind up more confused than ever.

Here are some of the good things about a dog and some of the drawbacks.

GOOD THINGS ABOUT A DOG	DOG DRAWBACKS

GOOD THINGS ABOUT A DOG

A dog is affectionate.

DOG DRAWBACKS

There is no way to get a grip on a dog so that you can give it a legitimate hug. You wind up hugging it around some delicate reproductive organ. Also, a dog is limited in the way it can express affection. The Lonely Guy who requires a variety of techniques will soon grow weary of the same old unimaginative licks and snuzzles.

A dog smells great.

Puppies smell fine. Old dogs don't smell that terriffic. But when it comes to dogs in their middle period, it's not that clear-cut. One of the toughest and most exhausting things to figure out is if a middle-aged dog smells all right or if it's a little off.

You can always figure out a dog.

On occasion, a dog will get a strange lopsided look on its face. It isn't hungry. It isn't thirsty. It just looks weird. This look may go back to a time when the dog had to get up at the crack of dawn and run around in primeval packs. Or it may not. Perhaps the dog just realized that it's a dog, and doesn't know whether it likes it or not. You can go crazy trying to figure out that look. In the long run, you'll just have to give up.

A dog is easy to feed.	A dog is never finished eating. Anything it eats is considered an hors d'oeuvre. If it were up to the dog, it would eat until it became an elephant. The dog assumes that any food brought into the house belongs to the dog. A pastrami sandwich arrives, it's for the dog. The dog feels hurt and betrayed when anyone else eats something. No one has ever successfully explained to a dog that people need nourishment, too.
A dog is alert.	A dog may be too alert. A dog can tell when bad news is coming, long in advance. If it were not for the dog, a Lonely Guy could enjoy himself, right up to the arrival of the bad news. But the dog won't have it that way. The dog knows when the Lonely Guy has been rejected or turned down for something. A dog even knows when there are parties going on that you haven't been invited to.
A dog is loyal to its master.	We assume that a dog is loyal to its master because of *Lassie.* But we don't know this for sure. Say you live in Apartment 14-H. One day, your dog accidentally wanders off the elevator into 10-H. The fellow there gives him unlimited

Gainesburgers, and to clinch the deal, throws in Alpo Swedish meatballs, which are irresistible to a dog (and don't taste bad to a person, either). It's a harsh thought to contemplate, but the dog may decide to tie on with the guy in 10-H and never give you another thought. Even though you have slaved over the dog and played fetch with him for fourteen years.

When you are dealing with a dog, there is always the lingering suspicion that if you're both trapped in a mineshaft for a week or so, the dog will start to eat your legs.

A dog will protect you from bad people.

A dog will protect you from wonderful people, too. It doesn't edit. If a person of the finest moral character shows up at your doorstep, the dog may behave as if the caller is Charles Manson, out on a work-release program. When great-looking women from Texas show up to collect for something, the dog may chase them away, too.

On the other hand, the dog may very well run right over and lick an embezzler.

A dog will attract women.

A dog will attract women to the dog. Not to you. These women are legitimately interested in the animal. They are not using this interest as a cheap ploy to get to meet you.

There is nothing lonelier than standing on the street with a collie that is surrounded by adoring women.

| A dog will never scold you. | Sometimes you *should* be scolded. Say you did something rotten, refused a date with a distinguished anthropologist because she had fat ankles. The dog will act as if you just did volunteer work in a hospital. When Hitler marched into Poland, the first one to congratulate him was his dog. Shouldn't *Blondi* at least have bitten the Führer on the ankle? |

A dog is easy to take care of.

A dog would be easy to take care of if it were not for the decision making. What exactly is a dog allowed to sniff at? How long should it be permitted to inhale building corner smells? If another dog bites your dog, should you encourage your dog to bite it back? Demand an apology from the owner? Hack at his neck? A great deal of mental strain goes into making these decisions.

A dog is easy to travel with. You just sit the dog up in the back of the car.

A dog sitting in the back of a car will remind you of a retarded niece in a Flannery O'Connor story who is being taken to a state institution.

Dogs have beautiful names.	Each time you call out the beautiful name . . . "Melissa" . . . "Heather" . . . it will remind you of the Melissa or Heather you are not allowed to have.
A dog allows you to feel superior.	Most dogs have better bloodlines than their masters. If you step out of line, the dog will give you a haughty look, a reminder that its forebears yipped along at the heels of Louis Quinze. And that you are a fellow from the South Bronx.
If you own a dog, you no longer have to sleep alone.	Dogs are terrible sleepers. A leaf falling in the next county will have the dog leaping out of bed and howling out the window. No one can snore like a dog. If a dog has nightmares, forget about it. Anything can cause a dog to have a nightmare. It doesn't have to be important. It might be a little piece of meatball that got away and rolled under the refrigerator. A dog will always take the most comfortable part of the bed, forcing the owner to sleep around the dog.
A dog will end your loneliness.	A dog may end your freedom, too. Once you commit to one, you can't play with it and then hang it up in the closet like a London Fog raincoat. It's always *there,* staring at you and reminding you of something you didn't do for it.

The Lonely Guy should think long and hard before signing on a dog. A dog is a bit of a Lonely Guy itself. And two Lonely Guys do not add up to one happy fellow.

One approach is to test-own a dog, borrow one and take it away for a weekend. Or perhaps accept a visit from your ex-dog, with the clear understanding that if it doesn't work out, the dog gets shipped back to wherever the hell it came from and not a peep out of it.

If a Lonely Guy can accept a dog's limitations—and not keep blaming it because it isn't a gorgeous immunologist—he can find a small amount of happiness with the dog.

Whatever his decision, he should not let himself get talked into a goldfish.

How to Take a
Successful Nap

He dozed off during an Army training film and was brought be-
fore his commanding officer, a Dutch reservist who normally sold
cars in St. Louis. "I don't want anyone in my squadron reported
for schleeping, understood?"

"Yes, sir," he said. And then, mimicking the Major perfectly,
so as not to be thought insubordinate, he said: "I'll never schleep
again."

"Are you making fun of me?" asked the Major.

"No, sir," he said.

"All right then. And no more schleeping."

On rare occasions, and against all odds, a Lonely Guy
will be spotted walking about with a cozy self-satisfied little
grin. What is his secret? The chances are that he is a successful nap-taker.

The nap has traditionally been maligned as a destroyer of
sleep. Let the Lonely Guy succumb to one and he will spend
the night staring at the ceiling, eyes seething with activity.
At its most diabolical, the Gestapo was unable to devise a
more effective sleep-killer than the fifteen-minute snooze.

This is an unfair charge. Naps can lead to other naps.
Experienced nap-takers can chain-nap their way along so that
there is very little of the day to worry about. The nap can

also serve as a drowsy little aperitif, whetting the appetite for a night of serious sleeping.

Not all men are gifted nap-takers. The secret of this art is doubtless one more piece of wisdom to be found scribbled away on the bulletin board of the all-knowing DNA cell. The average Lonely Guy cannot expect to make a sudden leap into World Class napping. By understanding the special nature of the nap, however, its whimsical ways, he *can* raise his proficiency and become a respected member of the napping community.

First Stage: Taking the Nap on Its Own Terms

The charm of the nap is that it cannot be planned with precision. Naps simply occur, unscheduled, unannounced, following a sleepy little drummer of their own. When a nap becomes possible, the untutored Lonely Guy will tear at his socks, hack away at tight underwear and may even issue a panicked call for an old childhood blanket. Before he can let out his first contented sigh, he will be more awake than ever—the frenzy of activity having made it impossible for the nap to take place.

In the same situation, the experienced nap-taker simply goes about his business—sharpening his scissors, polishing off a sonnet—pretending that nothing is up. He might be hooked over the arm of a chair or painting the bottom of a broom closet. No matter how uncomfortable his position, he will simply slump over and take his nap in peace, waving off the exaggerated dangers of circulation stoppage and possible amputation. In sum, the veteran nap-taker knows the fundamental napper's rule: Take the Nap on Its Own Terms. Do not try to reschedule it for a more convenient time—or reshape it to other needs. That will come later.

There is one exception to this rule: In rare cases, a nap will come over him when the Lonely Guy is in an authentically slippery position—stretched out of a high-rise window, waving to a college friend, or in the outer lane of the Pacific Coast Highway, in a Chevy Nova. In such cases, quite obviously, the Lonely Guy must shift over to safer ground. But he must also take exquisite care to *stay inside the nap.* At this stage, the nap is like a plate of hot soup. Spill one drop and the Lonely Guy may well be up for seven days and nights.

Second Stage: Securing the Nap

The second stage of nap-taking is hazardous precisely because it looks so easy. Once the nap has clicked in, the amateur tends to get cocky, rolling over with a happy yawn and assuming he is home free. The next thing he knows, he is sitting up in bed once again, saying: "Where did that sucker go?" This is because he has forgotten to Secure His Nap. The seasoned pro, on the other hand, grits his teeth, takes a firm hold on the reins, and in the only macho phase of nap-taking Shows the Nap Who's Taking it.

Third Stage—Downhill Napping

Once his nap has been secured, the experienced nap-taker is ready to settle in for some smooth sailing. To make sure there are no bumps along the way, he has done the following:

- Taken off his watch, one of the most important moves in nap-taking. A watch, during a nap, is ten times the bodyweight of the average Lonely Guy.
- Anchored himself down with a delicious snack, ideally a slab of pumpernickel with some cream soda so that the pumpernickel doesn't get lodged in there too firmly.
- Turned the radio to soft, innocuous music—so that he does not disco dance his way through the nap and wake up exhausted.

- Covered his feet, the most sensitive part of the body
  during naps, not with socks, a blanket or other toe-
  cripplers, but with a light and gentle garment, an
  old windbreaker—or the flag of a small Latin
  American country.
- Made a last-ditch sweep of his mouth, paying particular attention to lodged toothpicks and old forgotten macadamia nuts.
- Begun his nap in an awkward posture so that he can
  enjoy one of the napper's true delights—shifting
  over to his favorite position.
- Arranged himself so that he does not get couch
  button imprints on his back, which will have to be
  explained away.

Foot lightly on the brake, to avoid napping away an entire
month, the Lonely Guy is ready to enjoy the most satisfying time of all—Downhill Napping, sought after by nappers
the world over. Even at this pleasant juncture, however, the
Lonely Guy is not quite out of the woods. Nappers never
really are.

Here are some of the minor annoyances that might crop
up and how to deal with them:

- Overwide yawns which can lock in, yielding only
  to orthopedic skills. The napper must learn, reflexively, to smack himself when he feels one of these
  coming on.
- The phone. Archenemy of the nap. The Lonely Guy
  must decide quickly whether to answer it, or lie
  there twirling with indecision and killing off the
  nap. Established nappers have been known to carry
  on long conversations—and even make a grilled
  cheese sandwich—while still in the nap. The neo-
  phyte should not attempt this.

- Nap itches. The veteran napper, of course, scratches his in advance. Still and all, stubborn ones often slip by and should be handled with light, stroking, almost Zen-like motions, not clawed at with outrage. As for out-of-the-way shoulder-blade itches, the veteran napper prepares for these by keeping an object with an abrasive surface—such as a Brillo pad—in bed with him and backing his way up on it.

Final Stage: Milking the Nap

Toward the end of Downhill Napping, the Lonely Guy will hear a faint and distant sound, similar to a conductor's voice: "Ronkonkoma . . . everybody off for Ronkonkoma . . ." This is a signal that the nap is nearing its end. While freshmen nappers make a mad dash for the exits, the veteran simply rolls over sleepily and prepares for the Napper's Endgame, known by aficionados to have its own special pleasures and rewards. The hard climb is over, the battle has been won. All he need do is dig his head a little deeper in the pillow and Milk His Nap, enjoying the napper's "second cup of coffee." In the darkest of all worlds, he will go past the station. However, in the napping community, this is hardly a disgrace and may even be overlooked with a rascally wink.

Post-Nap Period

Once the nap has been accomplished and reentry successfully carried off, the napper who is new to the game will turn his thoughts to mouthwash, planning dinner, taking his sleep-rumpled clothing to the dry cleaners. Finally, he will begin to deal with the gnawing question that is so disruptive to all beginners: "How the hell do I get to sleep tonight?"

The professional napper—from his drowsy heights—will view all of this with amusement—and set about to do what every nap-taker worth his salt does: prepare himself for his next nap.

At the Beach

The father and mother were good at getting suntans. All they had to do was put their faces up to the city sun for a short while and they would get one. People would think they had just come back from a Caribbean island. They passed this gift on to their son who was fond of saying: "It's the finest inheritance a fellow could have." But secretly he wished they had left him a lot of money.

Every Lonely Guy needs fresh air, sunshine and a chance to get away from it all. The way to accomplish all that is to take an old-fashioned vacation at the beach. Some Lonely Guys who have tried the beach will scoff at the idea. They remember standing on the shore, staring at the horizon and getting a queasy feeling in their stomachs when they realized they were going to become part of The Great Beyond. The mistake they made was in assuming it was going to happen that very minute. Sure, they would *eventually* have to join The Great Beyond. That's part of the package. But it might not happen until Labor Day. Or, who knows, maybe not for a season or two. Meanwhile, they should have relaxed and had fun at the beach.

The way to pull that off is to abide by a few guiding principles.

Forget about How Much It Costs. Beach vacations have inched up in price since you were a kid and now cost a fortune. Only emirs can handle them comfortably. The Lonely Guy who shells out all that money will feel a certain pressure to run around like a madman, trying to have fun every second of the day. Since there isn't a hell of a lot to do at the beach (the whole *idea* of the beach is there's nothing to do there) a conflict may arise, causing dizziness and vomiting. Now, what's the point of having to be flown back from an expensive vacation, a whipped and dejected man, as a result of worrying about all the money you spent on it. Aren't you better off putting the money out of your mind and getting sick about it later?

Go with the Body You Have. When the Lonely Guy finds out he is going to the beach, his first impulse will be to make a desperate last-ditch try for a new body, possibly by doing heavy squats in a nearby gym. This is ridiculous. By the time you make a dent in your fat, it will be September, time to go home. A better idea is to Go with the Body You Have. And go the limit with it, too. That means parading around in a bikini, putting your belly on proud display instead of hiding it in tentlike shorts. The first one to adopt this style on an international scale was the great film director, Roberto Rossellini, to the scornful amusement of Jewish mothers throughout the land, who said, "Look at that *pippick* (stomach)." Yet he won Ingrid Bergman, *pippick* and all.

Never Step on a Person's Dune. A dune is a beach person's most sacred and valued possession. It's what keeps his house and his children and the whole beach from floating out to sea and washing up in Macao. Rap a person's kids, needle him about his ethnic persuasion if you must, but stay away from his dune.

The House You Live In

"A Few Houses in from the Beach." . . . The thing
about a beach house is that it's either on the beach or it isn't.
You don't get any points for being "just off the beach" or "a
few houses in." The fellow who is "a short jog away" is in
the same boat as someone who has to be brought in by
Concorde. Neither one is *on the beach*. A fellow explaining
how close to the beach he is is like a novelist telling everyone how much they love his book in England.

As a practical matter, make sure you are close enough to
the beach so that you actually get there once in a while. You
don't want to be a Lonely Guy on the porch, questioning returning travelers about the beach. (Not that *stories* about the
beach would be bad. What you would get then is the Myth
of the Beach, which might be better than the beach itself, like
Brecht's version of Alabama, a place he had never seen. But
at these prices, you really should get a taste of the actual beach.)

The Hateful Security Deposit. Even houses that are far
from the beach are terribly expensive because of the hateful
Security Deposit, the worst thing in beach vacations. That's
a huge sum of money paid to the homeowner in case you
smash up his house. If you don't smash it up, you're supposed to get the money back, which, of course, is laughable.

Beach houses are specially made to look sturdy and rock-
like upon examination and to fall apart at the touch the second you move in. Many were built by the same fellows who
construct fake buildings for Hollywood sets. A sound policy
is to kiss the Security Deposit goodbye, to consider it part
of the rental fee and not spend the whole summer planning
the fistfight you're going to have with the owner when he
won't return your money.

Cleaning. Even though a beach house will collapse when
you look at it too hard, it will be handed over in spotless

condition, with a stern warning that it better be just as clean when it's handed back. Many Lonely Guys get sick about this and start cleaning the second they move in.

This is ridiculous. Even if you trucked in batteries of cleaning ladies and had them working round the clock, you would never get the house clean enough to suit the owner. His sole objective is to hit you with a "cleaning fee" and deduct it from your Security Deposit. So relax about this one, too. You're not out there to clean. Do you want to remember your vacation as The Summer of Cleaning? Of course not. Enjoy the beach, and on the day you leave, tidy up some and get the hell out of there as fast as possible.

The Bargain in Garbage Disposal. The only thing that's cheap at the beach is Garbage Disposal. It's as if all the beach people got together and said, "Let's keep the price down on one thing." And that's what they chose. So even if you're a Lonely Guy who only plans to have a little bit of garbage, sign up for Garbage Disposal anyway. Since there's so little to do at the beach, you may decide to join the crowd that drives out to the edge of town each week and heaves their garbage in the dump. Even if you become part of that group, save some of your guck for Garbage Disposal so that you can take advantage of the low price.

Beach People

The Owners of the House. During the summer, you may get the uneasy feeling that someone is spying on you. It might be a mysterious car, cruising by at dusk, the driver craning his head unnaturally. Or a strange couple, peering at you from over a dune. This is not your imagination out of control, an effect of TV crime-show saturation. Someone *is* spying at you, the owners, trying to find out what you've done to their house. By mid-season, they won't be able to stand it any longer and will knock on your door, under the pretense that they were just in the neighborhood and wanted to see if you figured out how to work the dryer. Don't fall for this ploy. They are lying through their teeth. Invite them in for just one piña colada and you'll have an all-out war on your hands when they spot bacon grease on a slipcover. At the end of the summer, make sure you're safely on the highway before the owners take over the house. No law says you have to stand by with bowed head and be scolded for accidentally mangling a saltshaker.

Houseguests: Beware of Liv Ullmann. You'll be amazed at how easy it is to get houseguests to come out to the beach. As an experiment, call up the president of Gulf & Western, invite him out and watch him take the next private plane. Why shouldn't he? The house is costing you a small fortune and all he has to do is show up with a bottle of wine. So sort out your guests carefully. If Liv Ullmann shows up for the weekend, make sure it's *you* she admires, not the weekend. When you get back to the city, you don't want Liv dropping you like a hot potato.

Singles. Every weekend, a whole bunch of Singles will turn up at the beach. The way to get close to an attractive one is to strike up a conversation about how wonderful the beach used to be until all the Singles discovered it. Unfailingly, she will agree with you and think that you're charming, extricating herself from the other Singles.

Year-Rounders. Many Lonely Guys assume that locals, or year-rounders, are surly, resentful of summer vacationers and only tolerate them so that they can get at their money. This is a harsh attitude. Thanks to television and such social visionaries as Norman Lear, the whole country is now one big community. Rural America has seen such shows as *The Jeffersons,* too, which has taught the locals that *all* Americans have the same hopes and fears as they do.

As a result, rural folks can be counted on to wait until the last summer vacationer has departed before staging their Klan rallies.

One of the toughest romances to bring off is one with a local girl.

LONELY GUY: Can't we go out? This isn't Ulster, you know.

LOCAL GIRL: We're from two different worlds. There would be opposition from my parents, my relatives, my colleagues at the frozen yogurt store.

LONELY GUY: What if we met in the city?

LOCAL GIRL: Deal.

Things to Do at the Beach

Eating and Drinking. The great thing about beach eating is that everything tastes delicious out there. An old piece of celery you would sneer at in the city becomes an irresistible taste treat. A simple hot dog with mustard will have you rolling around on the floor in ecstasy. Before the day has gotten under way, Lonely Guys with frail appetites have been known to inhale half a dozen eggs and a box of sausages.

The best part about beach eating is that it will not make you as fat a guy as it would in the city. The same is true of drinking. The beach is an excellent time to try out all those off-trail drinks you wouldn't normally fool with—pear brandy, slivovitz, Mainland China Vodka, that kind of thing, none of which will make you as nauseous the next morning as they would in the city, either.

Some Cautionary Notes on Beach Eating: A thing to watch out for is sand. The Lonely Guy will spot some on a tomato and say, "Oh, what the hell, a little sand won't hurt me" and wolf down the sandy tomato. At the end of the summer, he's got a whole dune in his stomach, which won't come out that easily. . . .

Watch out for beach restaurants, especially ones offering gourmet meals, a contradiction in terms. Beach restaurants are notoriously inconsistent; they'll hit the heights with baked clams and send you roaring off in an ambulance with the roast beef. If you must go to one, order a grilled cheese sandwich, something they can pull off, and hold the line right there. Try not to get hungry for Chinese food, since the nearest Chinese restaurant is three hours away. If you know of someone who is driving out from the city, have that person save up the little white containers of leftover subgum and wonton soup from his last Chinese restaurant dinner and bring them out to the beach.

Don't get mad at bacon. There's something about the hot weather that gets people mad at it, for looking so nice in the package and then shriveling up to nothing. Bacon is bacon. It never claimed to be anything else. Try to enjoy it for what it is. . . .

Beach Movies. The beach is a great place to catch up on movies you wouldn't be caught dead seeing in the city. Films that are paralyzingly witless can be fun at the beach where you can hoot and holler at them to your heart's content. Many beach movie houses are fun in themselves, a bunch of chairs strewn about in an abandoned post office, giving you the feeling you're at a secret F.A.L.N. meeting. The two finest beach movies ever made are *The Wrath of God* starring Robert Mitchum and *Light at the Edge of the World* with Kirk Douglas and Yul Brynner.

Coming Up with a Philosophy. Most Lonely Guys scratch along from day to day and never give a thought to the Big Picture. They don't have a Guiding Philosophy to sustain them in their hour of need, which is every hour. The beach is an excellent setting for kicking around a few guiding philosophies and perhaps coming up with a winner. The best place to do this is at the edge of the sea. If you come up with one on a porch, it will be one of those Will Rogers cracker-barrel philosophies that won't stand up under real stress.

Once you're at the ocean, with the water lapping up against your shorts, you'll see clearly that all man's posturing and worrying is ridiculous since we're all just particles. That goes for everyone, from the most humble Chinese guy all the way up to Valerie Giscard D'Estaing, who, in the overall picture, is just another French particle. All particles eventually get shoved into the Eternal Stream, French ones, Hungarian particles, all of them. So isn't it ridiculous to worry about whether to put mustard or mayonnaise on a tongue sandwich, when we're all going into that stream?

In any event, that type of thinking, sharpened up a bit naturally, can stand as a philosophy. Trying to shape up a philosophy is a worthwhile activity, but take it easy when it comes to questioning the nature of reality. If you break through in that area, and prove, for example, that you're a prune Danish, and not an accountant, you'll be resentful about all the money you're spending on this vacation.

Volleyball. From a distance, this game appears to be a happy-go-lucky affair; in actuality, it is one of the most savage and crippling sports known to Western man. Houses have had to be sold, tight families have broken up, ad salesmen have torn down nets and walked into the sea—all because of volleyball arguments and slights. Fellows in rest homes stare at walls aimlessly because they were once chosen last on volleyball teams, or not chosen at all. Volleyball is a perfect game for the Lonely Guy who wants to cut his last civilized ties with his fellow man.

Most beach volleyball games have been going on for fifteen years and are impossible for a newcomer to break in to, the slots being passed along from father to son, like the stagehands' union. Your best chance to get into a game is to be on the sidelines when someone breaks a hip. But even when a newcomer gets into the game, he is still not in it since no one will pass the ball to him and for the first six summers he'll just stand there in isolation, the man in the iron mask.

Most volleyball arguments break out over whether someone has hit the net with his body, which is illegal; competition is so fierce that fellows accused of hitting the net have been taken to nearby laboratories to see if there are net strands on them. The basic unit in volleyball is made up of the "setter" and the "spiker," the former gently and lovingly lofting the ball up in the air so that the spiker can ram it down an opposing player's throat, ideally causing a disabling injury. The best way to earn a permanent place on the team is to become setter to a tall, ferocious spiker. This is very much like becoming the "girlfriend" of a tough fellow in prison who will see to it that no harm comes to you.

Getting Sick. The beach is not a bad place to be sick since beach doctors are surprisingly effective on anything up to a sore throat and will often bring off a cure where some lazy city doctor won't. The best thing about a beach doctor is that he isn't attending the Stuttgart Ballet, and you can actually get to see *him,* not his assistant. Beach drugstores are far ahead of the rest of the country when it comes to hay fever decongestants and the latest athlete's foot creams.

Worrying about Ants. Many Lonely Guys spend their entire vacation trying to figure out ant behavior. This is ridiculous since even the ants don't know what they are doing. Sometimes they come running out because a baked apple has been left uncovered. Other times, when all the food is wrapped up and in the refrigerator, they'll run out anyway and try to eat a best-seller. Ant intelligence has been overrated. They are not that smart. The individual ant has a tiny and unspectacular brain, even for an ant. It's only when a lot of ants get together and pool their individual routine brains that they become smart enough to carry someone off. Don't waste your time trying to dope out the ant's every move.

The beach is an excellent place for the Lonely Guy to go on vacation provided he lowers his sights and doesn't expect to have too much fun. He can have a little fun. Also, it's not a good idea to go out there every year; nothing marks the passage of time more dramatically than an annual visit to the beach, each summer another ring around the Lonely Guy's neck. It's better to turn up every five or six years and have the Passage of Time thrown in your face in one big gulp. For his other vacations, the Lonely Guy should go elsewhere, up North where he'll be too cold to worry about time passing—or to the Mediterranean, where it's the passage of French time and doesn't count in the same way.

Sex and the Lonely Guy

As childhood cousins, they played "Doctor," but, as the saying goes, they went no further. She had wet, smoldering eyes, and a forties' movie-star face. He lost track of her. Thirty years later, she showed up—at a time when he was having a puzzling but rich affair with a Chinese woman. He took his cousin to dinner and they went back to his apartment. Eyeing his bedroom, she said, "All these years . . . it's still the same."

"I'm sorry," he said, "but I can't handle a cousin and a Chinese woman at the same time."

Just because you're a Lonely Guy, it does not mean you've said goodbye to sex. Not by a long shot. There's tons of it out there, and it's your obligation to go out and scoop up some of it.

You're probably more interested in women than ever, the only question being how to proceed with them.

Men and women in the late Seventies don't have the slightest inkling of what to do with one another. Each sex looks at the other with a baleful eye. The slightest gesture, scratching an ear, or the most innocent question—"How are your tomatoes?"—is often misinterpreted as a hostile act. New translators may be needed between the sexes. Now that women are equal, they feel a bit awkward about it and wonder if they should have pushed so hard. Men would like to reach out and help but are afraid they will be smashed in the head. All men and women are miserable about this state of affairs, with the possible exception of Fritz Mondale. Exhausted, battle weary, women have gone off to take walks in the Poconos with their new friends—other women. Men sit alone in the dark and watch dart competitions.

Into this grim arena steps you, the Lonely Guy. What chance do you have for success with women? Considering your past record, you may feel the question is absurd. But is it, really! Though you tend to be a bit pale and green around the gills, you still retain a battered charm. You know failure. Rejection has been your friend. You are solidly grounded in ineptitude. Tired of being misunderstood, you've elected to be silent. This gives you the appearance of being a wonderful listener. These qualities will appeal to the discerning woman who does not reject you on sight.

This is not to say that lovely young women will be readily available to you. There is an abundance of them, but they are not all that easy to get at. In many cases, you will have to content yourself with seeing them pass in review beneath your windowsill, or disappear, heartbreakingly, into the arms of a Chilean. But you must continue to make a stab at getting some, no matter how thankless a task it seems. It's not essential that you succeed. Repeated tries will keep you in trim for that far-off day when you become A Lonely Guy No More.

What follows are guidelines for you, the Lonely Guy, in your bid for a slice of the sexual and romantic pie. If none seem applicable, remember that the greatest minds in history have fished in these very waters and rarely come up with a nibble.

A Basic Philosophy

Despite a scar or two picked up in the recent Great Struggles, women are more appealing than ever, warm, sensitive, caring, almost absurdly in touch with your feelings and theirs, able to spot a nuance at a hundred yards, an emotional tremor at a thousand—and more confident than ever about throwing these attractive features into play. Since this is true of *all* women, you might just as well try to get yourself a gorgeous one.

Categories of Women

Jewish Women. The big news is The Return of the Jewish Woman, or Jewish-American Princess, as it were. Many have been to Tibet. Others faithfully attend Masturbation Class. A lot of them kiss back. Some are enjoying rebellious second marriages to narcotics cops and reportedly do not snap and pick at them, demanding, for example, that they better their arrest records. The Jewish Woman is still a little tough, but it is a new kind of gentle and giving toughness. Don't write off the Jewish Woman. There is no need to run out and buy her a Mercedes—but give her an even chance.

Famous Women. Just because a woman is famous and successful is no reason to give up on her. We have all heard the stories. Candice Bergen sits home on Saturday nights. Cybill Shepherd, same thing. So when Saturday night comes around, call up Candice Bergen. The chances are you will catch her as she is about to go out—because all those stories are ridiculous—but at least you will have the thrill of having made contact with Candice Bergen and not having spent a Totally Lonely Saturday Night.

Much Younger Women. Don't be intimidated by Much Younger Women. Considerable nonsense has been written about the pitfalls of such relationships—the Middle-Aged Lonely Guy and the Much Younger Lovely Young Thing. There is only one real danger—younger women love to let out bloodcurdling screams, leap out from behind couches and pretend their heads have been chopped off. As a fun thing. They can't, for the life of them, grasp why you may find this offputting. If you can surmount this one obstacle, it's full speed ahead on women many years your junior.

Less-Than-Great Beauties. At a certain point, you may decide that you have had it with beautiful faces and bodies, that all of this is fleeting and transient and that only sound character is of importance. Once you come to this realization, and you *still* can't get anyone to go out with you, then you are really in bad shape. You must tread lightly at this juncture.

Actresses. No one can be more charming if you have a part for them.

Models. Good, when they hit age twenty-nine and realize they are not going to get away with their behavior forever.

Strategy and Tactics

Picking Up Women. Many Lonely Guys have reported great success in picking up women. Literally picking them up, right off the ground. This tactic has merit if it is not applied indiscriminately. It would not be wise, for example, to race over and pick up Lillian Hellman.

Horniness. Just because you don't feel particularly horny on a given occasion, there is no reason to stay home and sulk. On the contrary, go out of your way to schedule dates on Nights When You Are Not Horny. Women will appreciate this. "What a pleasure," your date will say, "not to have to be mauled and pawed at for a change." This relaxed atmosphere will tend to make her horny after a bit. And there is no rule that says you can't become Suddenly Horny, too.

Standing Pat. Many a Lonely Guy fails at romance because he is constantly trying to improve his hand. With a perfectly acceptable woman in tow, he will peer about at parties and Singles' Bars for someone Slightly More Delicious, and wind up going home alone. A good rule is to snap up the first person who pays the slightest bit of attention to you. In nine cases out of ten, it will turn out to be the best you could have done.

Be Yourself. Learn to be yourself around women. As a Lonely Guy, you may feel it's a bit risky, but it must be done, nonetheless. If you read *Hustler*, don't hide the latest issue in the bread box just because a woman is on the way. This approach can be overdone, however. There is no reason to leave heavy leather-bound volumes of *Enema Island* on display, just to show you have nothing to conceal.

Possessiveness. Never be possessive. If a female friend lets on that she is going out with another man, be kind and understanding. If she says she would like to go out with all of the Pittsburgh Steelers, including the coaching staff, the same rule applies. Tell her: "Kath, you just go right ahead and do what you feel is right." Unless you actually care for her, in which case you must see to it that she has no male contact whatsoever.

Taking a Shot. When you spot a lovely woman standing on a post office line or leaving Bloomingdale's, your normal impulse will be to think: "Oh, if she could only be mine," and leave it at that. Every now and then, it's wise to Take a Shot. Fall upon her with a great whoop and a goatcry and tell her how delicious she is and how anxious you are to take her to a restaurant. In almost every case, she will turn out to be living with someone, and desperately happy about it, but even this experience will not be wasted. Consider your little sallying forth as part of a series of practice rounds.

A Code of Honor. Never approach a friend's girlfriend or wife with mischief as your goal. There are just too many women in the world to justify that sort of dishonorable behavior. Unless she's *really* attractive.

A Weekend Game Plan. The worst dating time for the Lonely Guy is the weekend when the chances are he won't have one. An effective strategy is to schedule periodontal work on a Friday afternoon. This will keep you desperately uncomfortable until late Saturday night. At that point, you can say to yourself: "No sense calling anyone now. I might as well get the Sunday papers and pack it in." Simple as that, you'll be out of the woods. And you'll have tough gums, too.

Take a Meeting with Mom. Even in the New Culture, it remains true that the best way to tell how a woman is going to turn out is to meet her mom. So insist on Taking a Meeting with Mom. Your girlfriend may be the fairest flower beneath the sun, but if her mom looks like a utility infielder for the Montreal Expos, rest assured that your girl will eventually take on that Expo look.

A Most Desirable Relationship. Try to strike up a relationship with an ex-lover. The storm is over. Sex is out of the way. You can now relax, be friends, enjoy each other as people. Of course, these are terribly stimulating conditions, and you must be careful not to hop into bed again, in which case the whole business will become absurd.

New Bedroom Horizons

The New Erogenous Zones. One of the great breakthroughs in sex has been the discovery of all the new erogenous zones. Once it was thought there were only a handful. Now they are all over the place with new ones being reported every day. Don't try to go at too many at once. If you do, they will cancel one another out, with some of the traditional old-line ones being neutralized. A sensitive partner can help by tapping you on the shoulder and saying, "You are tackling too many erogenous zones."

Some of the newer ones are not immediately erogenous and must be cultivated a bit. It won't do to run over and start licking a knuckle, expecting erotic wonders. Later in the game, when the proper groundwork has been laid, that same laggard knuckle may suddenly turn tempestuous.

Dirty Talk. Women now freely concede that dirty talk is stimulating. Take this hint and start whispering a lot of it in your partner's ear. But make sure it's dirty. Halfway measures may backfire. For example, the line "I've always had great admiration for your labia minora" might very well have chilling consequences.

Orgasm-Spotting. There is no question that women love to have orgasms. But many women are confused as to whether they have been able to pull them off. You can be a good friend by helping to spot them as they turn up, hollering: "There's one right there" when a likely one is on the horizon. If your partner remains unconvinced, do not lose your temper and shout: "Goddammit, I know an orgasm when I see one." A much better tactic is to return patiently to the helm, and wait for a surefire one to loom into view.

In the case of some women, orgasms take quite a bit of time. Before signing on with such a partner, make sure you are willing to lay aside, say, the month of June, with sandwiches having to be brought in. It may be that you will prefer a partner with a quicker trigger, as it were.

The orgasm, finally, is a private experience. While one is in process, do not cry out, "Hey, what about me," and try to shoulder your way in on it. Though the experience may be a bit lonely, wait on the sidelines for it to blow over, at which time your patience will no doubt be rewarded and you will be ushered back onto the field.

S & M. As a Lonely Guy, you are probably familiar with lower back pain, and a host of other ailments. You may very well be a bleeder. Before joining in on the chic new S & M craze, make sure you sincerely want to spend an evening with a row of clothespins attached to your hips. You may decide in favor of a less elaborate alternative.

Surprises. Creativity is fine in sex. But try to avoid surprises. Unless you have announced it far in advance, do not suddenly reach over and pour a boysenberry sundae over your partner's feet.

Generally, it is a good idea to keep sex simple. If equipment has to be used, make sure it is bundled up in advance and kept alongside the bed. Nothing is more disturbing than to have to call things to a halt while you rummage through old cartons for a Pinocchio costume.

Role-Changing. No longer is there a stigma attached to changing roles in sex. If you feel a wave of femininity coming on, you can now safely lie back and enjoy it with no fear of losing your job in the State Department. But once having switched over, remember to switch back. Many Lonely Guys have made the switch and never been heard from again. It may be that you will want to set the alarm. The ringing of the bell will be jarring, but it will remind you to get back on that original road.

Three-Way Sex. The New Woman will very often, happily and lovingly, invite her girlfriend along for you to enjoy. All three of you will be expected to tumble into bed and there is no question that the experience will be tasty. But watch for the catch. The following weekend, you may be expected to haul out another male, so that your girlfriend can have a shot at him as well. Before embarking on three-way sex, be sure you are willing to make room in your bed for Roosevelt Grier.

Foreplay. Everyone loves foreplay, and you, as a Lonely Guy, should not avoid it. But don't get hung up on this activity, either. Egg rolls and spareribs are delicious, but they are not an end in themselves. At a certain point, it becomes time to push on to the Sliced Prawns with Black Bean and Garlic Sauce.

Positions. There is much to be said for the basic positions. The top one has a Conquering Hero flavor, just as being on the bottom brings along with it a certain Gandhi-like Strength. As a Lonely Guy, your best bet may be Sideways. When you are ready to call it a day, you will not be as tempted to leap off, gasping for air. All you need do is remain where you are and sink down for a quick chat, followed by a catnap. Added to this, Lonely Guys look their best from the side.

Final Word on the Clitoris. Once and for all, there *is* a clitoris. For a while, in the early Seventies, a theory took hold that it did not exist—that it was to be put in the category of Flying Saucers, with occasional sightings, none of them verifiable. Beyond the shadow of doubt, its presence has now been established, although it does tend to wander off now and then. In any case, the Lonely Guy must prepare himself to be on the lookout.

The Bonus. There will be times when you may not feel terribly sexy. "How can I be tumescent," you ask yourself, "when I'm a little down?" On those occasions, think of the middle linebacker who plays while in pain. The novelist who uses his gray periods to rip off best-sellers. The downcast actor who flies in from the wings.

And there's a bonus—your wailing sounds will be taken for passionate ones. An agonized teeth-gnashing grimace will slip by as a look of ecstasy. Cry out: "I can't take it anymore." Your partner will assume you're finding it all unbearably delightful.

Sex is too important to be sloughed off. Never before has so much of it been available to so many, including the undeserving.

It is your responsibility, as a Lonely Guy, and as an American, to go out and get some before it all goes away.

Epilogue
Whither
the Lonely Guy

He pictured himself, in years to come, sitting each day on the patio of the Gritti Palace in Venice and staring at the Canal. When tourists asked about him, the padrone would say: "He is the American. They say he once wrote very well and had extended correspondence with Alfred Kazin. He does not write anymore. He arrives here each day, orders a Negroni and waits for the Contessa who will not come."

As a Lonely Guy, you can expect to wake up one morning with a nagging lack of anxiety. Step outside and you will notice a discomforting bounce to your step. To compound the state of affairs, you will probably have a sense that all is right with the world.

Don't be alarmed. All Lonely Guys go through this experience. It is known as "free-floating happiness." It probably won't last.

Be patient. The chances are that before long that Comfortable Sinking Feeling will soon return. And you'll be back at the old post, leaning over railings, listening for the sound of foghorns, staring off in the distance and steeling yourself for the next off-trail development in your life.

No one, finally, can strip you of your loneliness. Into the world you came as a Lonely Guy. Out you will go, withered, a bit wiser, but pretty much in the same state. Loneli-

ness is a natural condition of life, as anyone who has ever
looked at a forlorn and bewildered amoeba under a micro-
scope can testify. Few, if any, make it to the Other Side. Most
are eventually driven back, like Norse invaders.

Isn't it possible, then, in some way, to stop dead on a dime
and become A Lonely Guy No More?

Sometimes life itself will lend a hand.

> LONELY GUY (opening door): Jeremy! What are you doing
> here?
> EX-SON (carrying a suitcase): Hi, dad. I heard you were
> lonely. I'd like to spend my last year with you
> before going off to Furman U.
> LONELY GUY: This is an awfully small place.
> EX-SON (entering): Don't worry about it. You'll hardly
> even notice me. Where do I put my collection of
> *Iggy and the Stooges* records?

Or else:

> LONELY GUY (opening door): Diana! What are you doing
> here?
> LOVELY REGISTERED NURSE (who altruistically ministers to
> the sick and the lame): I'm moving in. Don't try to
> stop me. I love you and I'm going to make you
> happy if it kills you.

Barring some such dramatic turn of events, most Lonely
Guys will have to pick their way through life on a day-to-
day basis, taking whatever cards life has dealt them and trying to bluff their way to happiness.

Don't fritter away badly needed energy in an attempt to
change your nature. You're a Lonely Guy! Get comfortable
with your loneliness. Whether you stay home with it, take
it out sailing or hold it aloft like a banner at the Cannes Film
Festival—enjoy it. Years later, you'll want to look back on

your Lonely Guy days as a rich and fascinating time of your
life, like the Army.

> HOUSEFUL OF GRANDCHILDREN: Tell us what it was like
> when you were a Lonely Guy.
> EX–LONELY GUY (now a Slightly Older Guy—with a sly
> smile): It wasn't bad. Not bad at all.

Bacon cheeseburgers, Cheryl Ladd posters, Ibsen revivals,
pine tar room fresheners, the scent of wisteria on another
guy's terrace—they're all out there for the Lonely Guy with
red blood in his veins and the courage to say: "I can have
these things, too, even though I happen to be living alone
for the moment."

Hats off and a fond farewell to you, Lonely Guy, as you
hunch those shoulders squarely, swallow hard, hang your
head medium-high—and valiantly set forth in pursuit of
your small but very own quite legitimate share of the pie.

The
Slightly
Older Guy

Illustrations by Drew Friedman

For Molly and Max—
Slightly Older Guys of the Future

Introduction
Who (or What) Is a Slightly Older Guy?

It takes him a little longer than it once did to get out of restaurant booths. But once he's on his feet, he stretches out a bit and breaks into the easy casual stride of a professional athlete, which he may never have been. He thinks about bran a lot. Is he getting enough bran? It seems that everywhere he goes he hears the word "pops" and assumes it's directed at him.

The Slightly Older Guy goes to pieces if someone criticizes his work, and he's become insecure about his appeal to women, even if (in the past) they've fallen at his feet. He worries about Trollope a lot. Shouldn't he be reading Trollope before it's too late? He's concerned that he may never see Kuala Lumpur, even though it has Burger Kings. He's tempted to write his memoirs, but is embarrassed because he's never slept with anyone famous. He hesitates before taking out a long-term auto lease for fear of being survived by a Mazda. And he wishes the medical establishment would make up its mind about the prostate. (Do something about it or leave it alone.)

If you wake up one morning with the sinking feeling that you're a Slightly Older Guy, don't panic. Not just yet. For one thing, you're in good company. Chevy Chase is a Slightly Older Guy and Bill Clinton is becoming one as we speak. Former Secretary of the Treasury Lloyd Bentsen may be out of the loop, but you have Rod Stewart for company, espe-

cially when he's singing and dancing with young rockers and is a little bit behind the beat. Dustin Hoffman has Slightly Older Guy written all over him, with all the attendant ramifications for his career. Howard Stern makes the list because of his serious concerns about his sexual organ, as does Robin Williams, if only he would sit still for a minute.

CNN is loaded with Slightly Older Guys, and NBC's Tom Brokaw, despite being winsome, has been one for some time. Warren Beatty, George Plimpton, Yasir Arafat, Candice Bergen (oops)—but why go on?

It would be nice to report that there are rich golden opportunities ahead for the Slightly Older Guy, but quite honestly very few come to mind. There's folk dancing, of course. If you're a folk dancer, you should be positioned nicely. But if you're part of the vast majority of Slightly Older Guys who don't folk dance, the territory you're about to enter is bleak and uncharted. Mistakes cannot be made. One stumble here and it's time for the fat lady.

What follows are some thoughts on how to survive this rough patch so that you're in decent condition when you break out into the clear and become a Considerably Older Guy—at which time you'll be sought out for your advice on the deficit and asked if we should go to war.

BJF

Water Mill, New York

(Division Headquarters for the Slightly Older Guy)

1995

Part One

Exploring
the New
Territory

Telltale Signs That You're a Member of the Club

"It's true I'm getting on a bit," you might concede begrudgingly, "but hold on a second. I'm feeling fine and I didn't have a care in the world until this subject came up. Before I start worrying, how do I know for sure I'm a Slightly Older Guy?"

To begin with, there's no point in worrying about it. Once you've crossed the line, there's no turning back, and worrying will only make it worse. But in case you need proof, here are some signs that you've become an official member of the club.

- *You're sitting at a bar* that's filled with attractive young people on their way home from work. You catch the reflection in the mirror of a fellow who is clearly out of place and wonder, with some irritation, why he doesn't push on to a watering hole that's more appropriate to his obviously advancing years. In horror you realize, hey, wait a minute, that's me!
- *You notice subtle changes in your body*—a slight sharpening of the elbows, an unwelcome latticework about the eyes, an odd new configuration of the knees. You can't quite put your finger on it—they're not exactly knobby—but they're not the knees you once knew and loved. Come to think of it, they don't perform as effectively as they once did—and your

physician has made a subtle mention of arthroscopic repair, quickly reassuring you that nose tackles have it done virtually every week.

- *You've had sex*—a week or so ago—and it's probably time for another go-round. It crosses your mind that maybe you ought to hold off for a bit—and ration it out, so to speak.
- *You run into a contemporary* you haven't seen in years and you're shocked by how much the poor fellow has aged.
- *On a bus,* you focus in on an attractive young woman and entertain thoughts about asking her out for a drink. She looks up, smiles, and says sweetly, "Would you care to have my seat?"
- *Your college alumni bulletin rolls in* and you note with discomfort that your class notes are sliding closer to the head of the list—a position you'd always assumed was reserved for a handful of hardy ninety-year-olds who were on hand when the college was first endowed.
- *It occurs to you that* you've been attending quite a few funerals recently—and that conversational topics like "quadruple bypasses," "organ transplants," and "hip replacements" are right up there with sports scores and the stock market.
- *You're forced to take aside a certain friend* who's only a few years ahead of you and ask him if he'd mind not prefacing his remarks with the phrase "Now that we're in the twilight years."
- *You find yourself sucking in your stomach* in public and notice that none of your pants fit comfortably. Rather than let them out, you loosen the belt a notch or two, keep the waist unfastened, and decide to change dry cleaners. Obviously, the one you have is shrinking your suits.

- *You make it through the night* without a trip to the bathroom and consider it a cause for celebration.

If all of this sounds familiar, don't worry, there's no need to lose it and start folding your tent. Once you've gotten yourself to admit manfully that you are, indeed, a Slightly Older Guy, the trick is to see this new phase of life as an adventure, with surprises popping up at every turn. Some, of course, will be unwelcome. But there are strategies for dealing with them, many of which will be set forth in the pages that follow—assuming that the author can still remember them.

Chin Fat

One of the first things you're going to have to deal with as a Slightly Older Guy is chin fat,* which generally rolls in overnight. You go to bed thinking, "I'll bet I'm one of the lucky ones who will never get chin fat," and the next morning there it is.

No one is immune. Not Paul Newman. Not even Robert Redford. Kevin Johnson of the Phoenix Suns will eventually develop some, and Clint Eastwood already has a fold of it, although his comes across as being sinewy and windswept. The critic Harold Bloom has literary chin fat; he may be hiding a small poet in there. The only people who don't have to worry about it are the Rev. Al Sharpton and pleasant moon-faced types who have had it their whole lives.

There is no need to drag Dan Rather into this.

Your first impulse when chin fat appears is to pat and slap it with the back of the hand in an attempt to press it down; then, with increasing frustration, to grab and yank at it. None of this is useful and may even serve to stretch it out a bit. (Happily, there are no recorded cases of people who've died from an overload of chin fat.)

The Good Fight

Chin fat is going to be with you from here on in, so you may as well get used to it. Here are some civilized ways for the Slightly Older Guy to cope with this unpleasant reality:

*A.k.a. rope neck, wattles.

- Instruct children that they are not to hop on your lap and tug at it—or, in the case of hyperactive youngsters, to take hold of it and attempt to swing back and forth.
- Advise young wives and girlfriends that it is not helpful to say, "Oh, I don't know. I think it's kinda cute."
- In public places, learn to whip your head around dramatically at intervals as if you've heard a gunshot. This will, for brief periods, flatten out your accumulation.
- Spend a great deal of time reclining on couches, with your head thrown back, staring languidly into space. This, too, will pull back your folds dramatically for as long as you can hold the position. (For guidance, refer to Truman Capote's early book jacket photos.)
- Grow a beard.
- The face-lift, of course, is an option, although there will always be someone around to whisper: "Don't you think he's done a remarkable job with his chin fat?" (Suddenly showing up in turtlenecks will not fool the observant.)

Finally, the philosophical stance is the only feasible one. There is no need to jiggle your chin fat about flamboyantly in the manner of the late film actor S. Z. "Cuddles" Sakall, but you might as well accept it. After all, isn't it just more of *you* to love?

Go with your chin fat.

Speak, Memory—Please

At some point, as a Slightly Older Guy, you're going to find yourself standing in the kitchen in your bathrobe, wondering *what on earth you're doing there.* Your first response might be to pound on the wall and cry, "For God's sake, why am I here?" Or, with moderation, to tap your temple encouragingly and prod, "Come on, pal. You can remember why you're in the kitchen. Give it a try."

Memory loss is an unsettling experience, but you're probably just overreacting. What you want to do is calmly take hold of yourself, put the whole business out of your mind, and as long as you're in the kitchen, make some productive use of the time. Dice up a cucumber, for example, or get rid of some old croissants. Once you've engaged in some such purposeful activity, it's likely that in no time at all you'll recall that you came into the kitchen for a liverwurst sandwich. It's possible you've forgotten to buy liverwurst, but that's a different issue.

Discouraging as such an experience may he, there's probably a simple explanation for it. You may have been preoccupied with some larger concern, such as whether we ought to take a stiffer position with the Japanese on barley imports or to throw our weight behind Crimea in its efforts to break away from Ukraine. Perhaps you'd been leafing through the *New England Journal of Medicine,* dipped into another one of their cholesterol diatribes, and decided to cut back on your liverwurst consumption. Or maybe you've just about had it with liverwurst.

Unfortunately, such explanations will be of little consolation to the Slightly Older Guy, who'll tend to be extremely sensitive about his memory. Cast the slightest doubt on his ability to recall and he'll snappishly rattle off a list of the Scottish kings. What he's forgotten is that his memory has always had a few gaps. How many times have you forgotten to pick up a gallon of milk on the way home? Or to come home at all, for that matter?

Was there ever a time when you could distinguish between Chita Rivera and Rita Moreno?

So You've Slipped a Little . . .

Let's allow for a moment that your memory isn't quite what it once was. How much of it do you require? It's one thing to forget a favorite shashlik recipe, but do you really need to remember the exact content of sixteenth-century papal bulls? Isn't it enough to recall their drift? Or perhaps to focus on the ones that annoyed Martin Luther? How often will you be called on to describe the battlefield at Tannenberg? Or to hold forth on Mameluke tactics at Ain Jalut? It's one thing to have a fund of anecdotes about Lenin's fear of hair loss, but what if you forget a few? Do you really think your friends will think less of you? Find some other way to amuse them. Buy them a drink for a change.

And let's say the entire siege of Malta suddenly vanishes from your mind, as if Malta had never undergone a siege. Will it make you less desirable as a dinner guest? It's highly unlikely. What's more probable is that with the obscure factual data gone from your mind, you'll find yourself running a leaner, tighter operation. Like Chrysler.

There's also the new Information Highway. Don't forget about that. With this baby running, all you need to do is slip into your study, boot up your system, and march out triumphantly with a full accounting of Turkey's naval strategy at Lepanto. That is, should your expertise be called into question.

Some Opportunities

If your memory has gone off by a hair, is there any reason why you can't use this alleged deficiency to your advantage? Let's say you've become confused about your accountant's number and somehow got Julia Roberts on the phone. Isn't it a perfect opportunity to strike up a conversation? Ask her about the competing demands of career and marriage—and whether she and her boyfriend have been able to adjust to the Hollywood community. There's no telling where such a conversation may lead.

Or what if you've set out on a trip to Atlanta and somehow ended up in Fayetteville? Instead of doubling back in frustration, why not stay right where you are and use the occasion to find out what makes the place tick? Just what is it that makes Fayetteville Fayetteville?

Thanks for Your Memory

For the Slightly Older Guy who continues to be upset about his forgetfulness, it's much more advantageous to think of your memory—although not quite as robust as it once was—as the good friend that it's always been, enabling you to forget dentist appointments and to remember forty dollars you stashed in an old windbreaker; to blot out entire failed marriages, yet retain in exquisite detail a night spent in the arms of a Sausalito folksinger; to forget you were ever described as an "ingrate" in a company newsletter and to remember instead the farewell dinner in your honor, one in which toasts were proposed to your sales record and you were sent off with a pair of monogrammed pajamas. In short, focus on a memory that's canceled out your defeats, highlighted your triumphs, and led you to think of your life for the most part as a series of happy events.

Above all, be grateful to the memory that enables you to forget now and then that you've joined the ranks of America's Slightly Older Guys.

Sex and the Slightly Older Guy

As a Slightly Older Guy, there's no need to say goodbye to your sex life, although it's true that you may have to make a few adjustments here and there. To put it in baseball terms, it's no longer realistic to rely on your high, hard one.

To survive in the romantic league, you've got to develop a slider.

Help from Your Heroes

As a younger fellow, all that was required of you was to show up—and the deed was half done. If you show up now—and that's all you do, show up—you may be asked to leave the premises. As a Slightly Older Guy, you'll have to call on all of your wisdom and experience to keep you in the game. And don't feel you're necessarily working at a handicap. Think of the great George Blanda, still kicking field goals in his forties; "Ancient Archie" Moore, a terror in the ring at fifty-five; Satchel Paige, racking up strikeouts at God knows what age. Don't think of these legendary figures while you're *having* sex—and certainly don't cry out their names for inspiration—but at quiet moments give some thought to them as role models.

The Old Pro

As a first step in moving to the next tier of your sex life, try to rid yourself of Performance Anxiety. The very word

performance is misleading. It isn't as if you have to trot out
on stage and play the ukelele. It's not like that, of course,
although once you're in front of the footlights you will have
to do more than just stare at the audience. Remember that
you have considerable experience in this area—probably
more than you recollect—and it isn't just a matter of having once mastered erotic toe manipulation in the Philippines.
For example, there are no doubt a wealth of erogenous zones
you can call to mind if you take a minute to think about them.
Write them down and you'll be amazed at the length of the
list before you even get to the inner thigh. And each of your
lovers has probably passed along a trick or two which you can
call into play with your current partner—although there's no
need to credit your source when you do. When your bed partner sighs and says, "That was wonderful," don't tell her you
learned it from a saleswoman at Neiman Marcus.

If you can summon the energy, you'll find that even as a
Slightly Older Guy you're a whole bundle of sexuality.

Here are a few fundamentals you might want to give some
thought to before you get under way.

LIGHTS, MUSIC!

Generally speaking, lights should be warm and nonthreat-
ening. Harsh fluorescents will put your partner in mind of
a gynecological checkup. Admittedly, this can be arousing
now and then, but to be on the safe side, keep the lights low.
(Besides, as a Slightly Older Guy, you don't want your lover
getting too good a look at your waistline.)

EYES LIKE DEEP POOLS

The most formidable of defenses will crumble under a hail
of flattery. Keep your complimentary remarks personal.
Direct them to hair, perhaps, or fragrance, but not necessarily to decorating skills. And you don't want to make too

much of your partner's lovemaking experience or draw
undue attention to specific body parts.

As a rule of thumb, and provided compliments are framed
tastefully, you can't fire off enough of them.

VARIETY

It may be that your presentation has become predictable and
it's time to approach your lover from a different direction.
If so, it will add more spice to the experience if you don't
announce your plans in advance. Capitalize on the element
of surprise.

And vary the locale now and then, although as a Slightly
Older Guy it is wise to select a soft surface, wherever it
might be.

You might try sex with your clothes on now and then.
Or even switching clothes as long as there's general agreement beforehand that all items are to be returned to their
original owner.

FANTASIZE

A standard method of adding savor to your lovemaking is
to imagine that your partner is someone else—Sharon Stone,
Bridget Fonda, Margaret Thatcher, anyone you're not in bed
with at the time. Or imagine *you* are someone else—Judge
Ito if you really want to get wild. No one's checking up on
you. (A line should be drawn at Helmut Kohl.)

For a truly great stimulant, you might want to try a little-
used formula which involves thinking of *the person you're actually making love to.* But don't overwork this approach. It is
only effective if it's used sparingly.

BE YOURSELF

The best way to behave in bed is the way you behave out of
it, which is what got you into bed in the first place. Don't

assume an entirely different personality just because you happen to be naked. You may be a Slightly Older Guy, but *you're* the one who's been chosen as a lover, not Danny DeVito.

Positions: Scaling Back

The Slightly Older Guy who's accustomed to working with thirty or forty positions should think in terms of reducing that number to half a dozen or so. Eliminate those that involve a great deal of thrashing about and call for strenuous hip and leg movements. Also ones that require the use of some overhead appurtenance to keep your balance. Ideally, you want to keep the positions that offer maximum comfort and support so you won't do any permanent damage to your lower back.

A Salute to the Big Fella

A word here about your equipment, or the Big Fella, as you may have generously dubbed him after a successful romp in Tijuana many moons ago. It isn't as if he's been off on his own all these years. He's been with you through every campaign, a close and valued member of the team who's stuck by you through thick and thin, which is more than you can say for some of your friends. He may have faltered here and there, but he's never given less than his all in your behalf. And on those few occasions when he's gone on furlough, he's soon returned cheerfully to the fray. He was there with you at your first dance, every bit as tremulous and uncertain as you were, and stayed on even though there were times when he arrived at the front, ready to do his duty, only to discover that his services were not required, forcing him to retire to the barracks in frustration.

He's shared the strenuous and rollicking days of your youth, when he was asked to go forward blindly into unfamiliar and bizarre situations. He's with you now, at a presumably more peaceful time, just as loyal as ever but perhaps a bit weary now that you've become a Slightly Older Guy. Hasn't he become a Slightly Older Guy, too? Just be patient and don't expect more from him than you yourself can deliver. Treat the old boy with kindness and respect. When the bugle calls, you may be surprised to find that he will rally round and march proudly at your side, once again bringing honor to your banner—the banner of a Slightly Older Guy who's still very much in the parade.

Insults and Rejections

As a Slightly Older Guy, you'll find that your feelings are much closer to the surface than ever before. An unreturned phone call, the failure of a headwaiter to greet you with ceremony, a young woman addressing you as "Sir" —any one of these occurrences will be enough to plunge you into despair. You may start thinking someone's out to get you. But you've merely become a victim of heightened sensitivity. Let's not forget. You're a Slightly Older Guy. It goes with the territory.

Here are some touchy areas—and some strategies on how to cope with them.

"Why Him and Not Me?"

The success of a friend or contemporary, once a minor nuisance, will now come across as a personal affront. Be careful that your response isn't disproportionate. Don't start resenting an engineer friend's appointment to adviser of the shuttle program and forget that your own background is in dinette fixtures. Or become annoyed at Joe Pesci for being chosen over you as Best Supporting Actor at the Academy Awards when you've never been in front of a camera and Pesci has been slaving away at his craft for years.

Pesci may have gotten wind of some of *your* achievements. Maybe he's heard that you were named entertainment director of your condo and he's upset about *that.* More important is that Pesci wasn't given the Oscar just to make you feel awful. The members of the academy have probably never heard of you. (And don't let that set you off.)

The main thing is to forget Pesci and get some kind of life.

Don't Push It

When it comes to women, the Slightly Older Guy may find himself becoming particularly thin-skinned. If a woman flirts with him, it won't for a second occur to him that she finds him attractive. His first impulse will be to get out of town before she comes to her senses. Or, at the other extreme, he'll start to behave too aggressively, marching up with unnatural boldness to beautiful women. And when, for example, supermodel Elle McPherson politely declines his invitation to go to Barbados for the weekend, he is absolutely certain she's turning him down because he's a Slightly Older Guy.

Here again, a little detachment is in order. For one thing, Elle McPherson might not care for Barbados. Maybe it's just not her scene. Or it may be that she's been there on so many shoots that Barbados is coming out of her ears. Or perhaps she's got something going with Brad Pitt and wants to see how it plays out before she makes any new commitments.

"That's all very nice," you might say to yourself, "but if I was a young guy, I'll bet she would've hopped right on that plane."

Not necessarily. Even if that were the case, she might have wanted to find out just a little bit more about you. Give McPherson some room and she might surprise you by coming round. And if for some reason she doesn't, you can always try Claudia Schiffer.

The Restaurant Challenge

The restaurant is an arena that's sure to test the Slightly Older Guy's ego. Touchy to an extreme, he'll stride into a

four-star restaurant and demand to be seated at Woody
Allen's table, even if the legendary filmmaker is right there
in the middle of his dinner.

If you've been behaving in this manner, you're definitely
out of line. What you've got to realize is that even though
you've seen all of Allen's pictures and have been supporting the man for years, he may not *want* you at his table on
this particular evening. Maybe he's entertaining some
friends from out of town. Or trying to get Daniel Day-
Lewis to work for scale in his next picture. You can't expect him to make room for you because he doesn't want to
hurt your feelings. Take the high ground and accept a table
next to Allen's where you can wave to him now and then
and occasionally lean over and offer some opinions about
cinematographers.

"I'll Get Back to You"

The failure of a friend or colleague to return a call immediately is a fact of life—but not to the Slightly Older Guy
who'll no doubt see it as further evidence that the cards are
stacked against him. Yet there are any number of reasons
why your call hasn't been returned. Maybe your friend has
had an attack of laryngitis. Or he's busy fending off a sexual
harassment suit. If he's an agent, it's possible he's left for
another agency.

Don't sit around and brood about any of this. Make an
omelette while you're waiting. Sandpaper something or start
reading *Middlemarch*. If he hasn't returned your call in twenty
minutes, arrange to be unavailable when he does finally get
back to you.

Where's My Invitation?

Inevitably, you'll hear of a party to which you haven't been
invited.

"That's it for me socially," you'll conclude sadly. "No one wants a Slightly Older Guy hanging around and dampening the festivities."

There are any number of reasons why you might not have gotten an invitation. Here are just a few:

- *Someone you hate* is going to be there, and the host, out of respect for your feelings, has removed you from the guest list.
- *You're being saved* for a more important party, in honor of Morley Safer.
- *You did get an invitation* but the doorman intercepted it. He's over there now, living it up.
- *The host knew of several other competing parties* and took it for granted you were unavailable—not realizing you weren't invited to those parties either.

Just don't sulk and carry on about this. Plenty of other parties will come along. Sooner or later everyone is invited to *something*.

On-the-Job Sensitivity

It's conceivable you'll survive rebuffs from fashion models and headwaiters, but the inevitably sly comments about your work are going to sting. Suddenly you'll be told that your drawings aren't "edgy" enough, or maybe that your last presentation to the dairy farmers lacked a certain contemporary edge. Try to stand firm. There's a strong chance it's just part of a campaign to get you to lower your price. If they're in a jam and no one else is available, you'll be told your work has taken on a new freshness and vitality.

The Ten Best . . .

Sooner or later, a list is going to be published that you're not on. A list of achievers, people who live in the Hamptons,

people who were at some terrific party while you were at home, brooding. Slightly Older Guys are particularly vulnerable to not being included on lists. The way to deal with this is to make it known that you're not interested in lists and that, frankly, you have some questions about the people who make them up. You've heard it's possible to *buy* a place on certain lists, so do they really mean anything? Besides, you're on the only list that really matters—the one that's in the hearts and minds of the people you really care about. If you finally get on one of those socially significant lists, say you're enormously flattered but that you're *still* not interested in them. That's in case you're not on the next one.

Remember that not even George Plimpton makes every list.

Part Two

Shaping Up

A Diet for the
Slightly Older Guy

There's no reason to make any drastic changes in your diet. As a Slightly Older Guy, you still need a substantial breakfast to get you off the ground, assuming you're going to get off the ground at all. Generally, it will come down to juice, toast, cereal, pancakes, bacon, and the like in one disappointing combination or another.

If you're frustrated by this tired fare, one way to shake up the dice is to change the order of your meals. This is not to suggest that you kick off the day with couscous and flaming shashlik. But a modest helping of liver and onions in the morning can make for a refreshing change. If you're concerned about the long-term effects of missing an occasional breakfast, you can always polish off a bowl of oatmeal before turning in at night.

The Egg Makes a Comeback

A major innovation in the breakfast arena is in the preparation of eggs. Once feared by the Slightly Older Guy, the egg, when stripped of its yolk, can be consumed in large quantities and is guaranteed to go whistling cleanly through your arteries. Prepared in this manner, eggs even taste a little like eggs. So now might be a good time to revisit this old favorite. Remember, however, that inserting chunks of Polish sausage into an omelette isn't going to help your cause in the least.

Watching Your Weight

Weight control is of particular importance to the Slightly Older Guy. At one time, you may have been able to wave off hip fat, but this is no longer the case. And nobody loves a Slightly Older Guy who's also a Slightly Chubby Guy (a.k.a. a Person of Weight).

Here are some ways to make a dent in those excess pounds.

WATER

Keep water around at all times, and whenever you feel a hunger pang pour out a glassful. You don't have to do this in elevators or on street corners. But keep a pitcher of water in your office and on your night table. Those who've switched to water diets are reported to be thin and clear-eyed, although somewhat fidgety.

HALF A SANDWICH

A novel approach to diet is to prepare any dish you like and *eat only half of it.* Slightly Older Guys have enjoyed great success with this program, their only question being what to do with the other half. Unless you've disposed of it, you're going to find yourself making wistful trips to the kitchen and wondering whether or not to snatch it out of the refrigerator.

One solution is to eat the desired half and feed the remainder to your pet—unless, of course, he's a Slightly Older Dog who is also watching his weight.

Miami restaurants have joined in the spirit of this new movement by serving sandwich halves and withholding the second half, which is reserved in your name and can be picked up the following day. It should be noted that half a Miami sandwich is equal to a whole one in flinty Vermont.

IGNORING THE CLOCK

Another useful dieting measure is to stop being a slave to the clock. Just because it's twelve-thirty, it doesn't mean you have to eat something. There's no one watching you and saying, "It's lunchtime, grab a sandwich or face serious consequences." We're not dealing with a gulag situation here. If you're not hungry, put food out of your mind and do some work for a change. You can eat your meatball hero half an hour later and have all those extra minutes of dieting to your credit.

Foreign Fare

As a Slightly Older Guy, you don't want to spend your precious evenings slaving away over a hot stove. It's important to get out and about and try some of the great new ethnic food that's all over the place.

A few suggestions:

JAPANESE FOOD

Japanese restaurants have become a great favorite and are an excellent way to make social connections. All kinds of fascinating people sit at sushi counters. Your neighbor can turn out to be a Canadian tentmaker—or the owner of another Japanese restaurant. In this relaxed atmosphere, not only will you find yourself making friends, but you'll also be offered all those little pieces of squid that the individual beside you hates.

One of the great attractions of Japanese food is its artistic preparation. It's so beautiful to look at that very often you won't have the heart to eat it, which is in itself slimming. A word of caution, however, about sashimi. Raw fish has been proven to be sexually enhancing and you want to resist the impulse to pinch the waitresses on your way out.

CHINESE FOOD

Chinese food, too, has its allures, although it's not so much the General Tsao's chicken and the thousand-year-old eggs as the conviviality of the staff that makes the dining experience appealing. The warm greeting of a headwaiter ("Welcome back, Mr. Dinsmore. Long time no see") will make you feel you're a turn-of-the-century freebooter in old Shanghai.

STEAKHOUSES

Steakhouses had fallen out of favor, but are miraculously becoming chic again. Most gangland rubouts take place in such restaurants, which creates a not altogether unpleasant sense of danger in the air. As you dig into your porterhouse and baked potato, there's always the chance that someone in the next booth is going to be slaughtered.

SOME ADVISORIES

Stay away from restaurants that bill themselves as the "Oldest Dining Spot" in town—since they may be serving old food. And the great Nelson Algren's dictum still holds up: "Never eat at a place called 'Mom's,'" with an occasional exception. If your mom is the chef, for example.

Don't Forget the Classics

As a Slightly Older Guy, you'll naturally want to see and do it all before the lights get any dimmer. "What's life," you might find yourself asking, "if I've never tasted flamingo haunches or baby goat patties in sweet-and-sour sauce?"

This is understandable, but in reaching out for the exotic, you don't want to turn your back on old favorites that have gotten you to where you are—whether you're pleased about this or not. Take a moment to pay your respects to the banana, for example, which never quite made it as an ice-cream flavor but at least is still reliably a banana; to the apple, which is also boring but makes up for it somewhat with its cheerful appearance. Tip your hat to the olive, in all its weird-ness, to the cucumber for its stubborn efforts to be interest-ing, and to lettuce—you know, the old kinds, before the onset of radicchio. Raise your glass to calm, transforming mayonnaise, to the grape, mercifully divested of its seeds, and to the celery stalk, considered worthless by many but proud and magisterial all the same. Pay a tribute to Swiss cheese, relegated to the back of the bus by many, but still royalty to a few diehards; to the unique tomato, if you can find one that tastes like a tomato; and to toast, simple toast, which has seen you through many a queasy stomach—more than you can say for cappellini in lime marinade.

And finally, salute garlic, great garlic, proof if anyone ever needed it that yes, there is a higher power.

Your Body—and Its Message

As a Slightly Older Guy, you know your strengths and weaknesses at the dinner table. Treat your stomach with respect but not servility. Cater to an occasional whim if you must—a slice of pepperoni pizza won't seriously shorten your life span—but don't cave in to a craving for fried calamari at bedtime. And if you lack the will to do so, take your ant-acids beforehand. Some of the new lemon-flavored ones are so satisfying you may end up forgetting all about the fried calamari.

The rules by now are evident: Don't eat while you're chas-ing a bus. Feel around for bones in your flounder. Shake the sand out of your spinach. When dining out, stick with the specialties. If a restaurant calls itself Davy Jones and has a photograph of a fish in the window, it's trying to tell you something. Don't order the corned beef and expect it to amount to much. Eat one meal at a time and don't start planning the next before you've gotten past the appetizer. Chew your food, of course, but don't forget to swallow it. And listen carefully to your body. If it asks for baked ziti, get some in there as soon as possible. The same is true of smelts. If it cries out for smelts, give it smelts. And don't accept any of the smelt substitutes.

There are many dining treats on the horizon, hundreds for all you know. Proceed cautiously, avoid jalapeño peppers, and there's no reason why you can't play out your hand in comfort as a well-fed Slightly Older Guy.

Earrings and Ponytails

There may be a cloud or two gathering up ahead, but that's all the more reason not to neglect your appearance. Only the truly discerning will be able to look past battered loafers and a jacket covered with soup stains to see the real you—which you may not want to reveal in any case.

"What about Albert Schweitzer?" you might ask. "He didn't care how he looked."

That may have been true of Schweitzer, but the chances are you're not going around collecting prizes and attending conferences on humanitarianism. If you are, then you might not care what you look like either. But remember, Schweitzer is said to have done poorly in cocktail lounges.

Forget Schweitzer. Concentrate on sprucing yourself up a bit.

The Great Earring Question

A question you might as well address right up front is whether you want to try an earring. At one time, this may have seemed an affectation, but now that accountants and captains of industry show up with them, you're liable to feel left behind if you don't pop one in.

A great fear has always been that if you wear one, someone is going to beat you up—but the very people who once concerned you are now parading around with earrings of their own, and starting to worry that you might beat *them* up.

If you decide to get an earring, the worst-case scenario—and it's not all that bad—is that you'll run into an unsavory type who's also wearing one. There may be some wary circling about in the street—you might Mace each other up a bit—but the chances are you'll go your separate ways, or who knows, even end up at the same party.

Once you've committed to wearing an earring, you'll have to decide which ear you want to put it on and exactly where on the ear you want it placed. It's no secret that the positioning of an earring can indicate sexual preference. But it can also signal anything from animal rights activism to support for the Tamil minority in Sri Lanka—and you might not have strong feelings about either cause. So do your research.

For starters, at least, you'll want to select an earring that's small and inconspicuous, although not so small that people will strain to see if it is indeed an earring or a pimple. Avoid giant tire-like affairs that are not only attention-getting but will also weigh you down to one side, potentially causing dizzy spells.

For your first public appearance, you can deal with your insecurity by either revealing the earring gradually, cupping one hand over it and giving peeks at it to an occasional passerby, or by storming into a waterfront bar, ordering a boilermaker, and flaunting it boldly at rowdies.

After several outings, you'll find it's become part of your look. Rarely will someone cry out, "Here comes the guy with the earring."

Once you've settled in comfortably as an earring person, there'll be a temptation to balance yourself off with a second earring—but this can lead to nose studs and metallic appendages on other body parts, and you may not want to go in that direction.

Stick with the one earring. Then give some thought to your hair.

Hair Today . . .

Hair plays a tremendous part in contemporary life. There's no question that Clinton's hair swung the election in his favor.* Does anyone doubt that Gorbachev would still be in power if it weren't for Yeltsin's great hair? You have to go back to Eisenhower to find a bald President, and that's because Adlai Stevenson had even less hair than Ike did.

Small wonder that the Slightly Older Guy is deeply concerned about his thinning and perhaps graying locks.

One way to deal with this is to use one of the many products that are designed to change your hair color overnight. If you're sensitive about trying one, you can always apply it in a small border town where no one knows you. If it doesn't work out or causes a stir, even in the small border town, just stay put for a month or so until it all grows out; then return home with your old hair and no one will be the wiser.

A toupee is another solution, but if you choose this option, make sure to stay with a top-of-the-line product and not just any old kind that's on sale at Woolworth's. Ask Tony Bennett where he got his. You don't want people poking each other and saying, "Did you see the rug on that guy?"

As to the rumor of a magazine in the works that "outs" bald people who wear hairpieces—there's no truth to it. You can relax on that score.

The Ponytail Decision

Inevitably, with the example of youth swirling all around you, you'll want to consider wearing your hair in a pony-

---

*Bush had hair, too, but it was that thin preppy kind which is not a vote-getter.

tail—assuming, of course, there's enough of it left. The Slightly Older Guy who grows a ponytail often does so in the hope of trimming years off his age, and with luck, being taken as the lead guitarist for Blind Melon. More specifically, a ponytail is designed to swing the focus away from your baldness, although this can backfire and call attention to your upper-back hair. Try to keep this unpleasant growth covered.

Ponytails are not appropriate for every profession. It's one thing for them to be mandatory at TriStar; it's quite another to imagine Secretary of State Warren Christopher wearing one as he strolls up to the microphone to announce a change in our stance toward Macedonia.

If you decide to go ahead with a ponytail, keep it at a modest length and neatly tied back with a rubber band. There have been tragic deaths involving commodities brokers who got their ponytails caught in elevator doors.

Above all, keep your hair clean. Nobody admires a Slightly Older Guy who looks like Howard Hughes.

A Wardrobe Update

With your earring and ponytail accounted for, you'll want to pay some attention to your wardrobe, which may be sadly out of date. A difficulty here for the Slightly Older Guy is that men's clothing never seems to wear out—with the exception of today's socks, which shrivel up into little balls after a use or two. Rather than discard a perfectly serviceable sports jacket, the Slightly Older Guy will stubbornly continue to wear it, even if it dates back to the Truman administration. At a certain point, however, you may decide—or the Board of Health may decide for you—to get rid of your old clothing, which may not be as easy as you think. Even the Salvation Army has to draw the line somewhere.

In pruning down your wardrobe, don't be overly aggressive. Keep in mind that certain items are capable of making a comeback. This has already happened in the case of Nehru jackets. And there's hope still for your collection of skinny ties.

The Slightly Older Guy "Look"

With space in your closets, you'll be ready to make a few modest purchases. But just because you haven't shopped for a while, there's no need to buy out the whole store. Some trousers and a jacket or two, deftly switched around in various combinations, can quietly establish you as a clotheshorse.

194

Sometimes a single item can make a world of difference. A Versace tie, for example, with the right combination of fruit and palm trees painted on it, can result in crowds of the curious gathering around you at cocktail parties.

The bright side? As a Slightly Older Guy, you don't have to worry about wasting money on clothes that will "last you a lifetime."

The Well-Scrubbed Look

To secure your precarious footing as a Slightly Older Guy, you'll want to pay special attention to hygiene. Nose hairs should be trimmed off at the pass, and unless you play the guitar, you don't want to be seen with long fingernails. Although they are rarely credited with doing so, hairy ears have been known to choke off many a budding romance. So make sure to deal with that problem.

An entire industry exists to cope with your breath, so there's no excuse for any slipup here. America has the best breath of any country, and you'll want to do your part in keeping it that way.

Soap, teeth whiteners, deodorants, wrinkle creams, mustache darkeners—they're all out there for you, and there's no excuse for not taking advantage of them. There are obstacles ahead—who could possibly argue with that?—but you'll be better able to face them as a well-groomed Slightly Older Guy.

At the Baseline

With your diet in order and your earring and ponytail in place, you want to make sure that you're a picture of fitness. As a Slightly Older Guy, you'll find that tennis is an excellent conditioner since it can be taken up at any time no matter how far along the road you've traveled. Benefits include a trim waistline and a belly that's been reduced in size so that there's no longer any need to disguise it with caftans. Time, unfortunately, may already have thinned out your legs; still, no matter how spindly they've become, some vigorous play on the tennis court should provide a bit of shape to them.

If you're a beginner, before you go charging out onto the courts it's advisable to invest in a lesson or two. There are a bewildering number of approaches to the game, and instructors vary wildly in their recommendations.

THE BALL

Some argue for making the ball the centerpiece of your game and keeping a watchful eye on it at all times. Others claim that watching it alone is of little value; what you want to do is make guesses as to its eventual whereabouts so that you can be on hand to greet it. Yet another school insists that it's not so much the ball that should be studied as it is your opponent's feet, although obviously not in lustful fascination.

THE NET

There's disagreement, too, as to what attitude to take toward the net, other than whacking it with your racket in frustration. Some recommend avoiding it at all costs; others encourage charging up to it fearlessly when given the slightest opportunity. A third group advocates approaching the net, though somewhat warily, and only after Building a Case, in the fashion of a prosecutor gathering evidence for an indictment.

Once the player has arrived at the net, however, there's a general consensus that the racket should be positioned so that it shields the genital area. Unsportsmanlike though it may appear, it's not unheard-of for a diabolical opponent—in the hope of winning a match by default—to unleash a disabling shot in that direction.

STROKES

As for strokes in general, some advise lashing out with fury at every ball that comes your way. Others feel the wise course is to conserve energy, hitting the ball modestly until your opponent begins to tire and only then striking out with conviction. Players have been known to wait years for such an eventuality.

All schools agree that the novice should keep the ball in play long enough *to allow his opponent to be the one who commits the blunders*—and not leave the court in tears when this fails to happen.

As for particular strokes, you'll find instructors becoming lyrically extravagant in their advice on how to execute them. In attempting a backhand stroke, you'll be told to reach round in back of yourself and pull at the racket "as if you're unsheathing a bowie knife." As for the forehand, the trick is to swing through the ball and finish off the stroke by "shaking hands with yourself," although not necessarily in a congratulatory manner.

THE SERVE

The first serve is of great importance and should be delivered with authority. The second is another matter. Ideally, it should have some novelty to it, a coquettish little spin, for example, designed to overpower your opponent with its charm.

FEAR

After a number of lessons, you may experience a Fear of Actually Playing. But as a Slightly Older Guy, with time not necessarily working to your advantage, you need to get on with it. Put your lessons behind you and step out on the court, ready to do battle. Before doing so, it's essential that you have at the ready the most important weapon of all.

The Excuse for Poor Performance

As a Slightly Older Guy who's never played before, you're ideally situated in this regard. You can trot out on the court and declare in all candor, "I've just taken up the game." Or if you've played a bit as an undergraduate, heft the racket, look at it ruefully, and say, "Amazing. I haven't picked up one of these things in years."

Another successful gambit is to limp out on the court and say with a wince, "We can *try* a few points. I just hope the knee holds up."

The surface, too, can be blamed in advance as an excuse for poor play ("This is my first time on clay"), as can knavish behavior the night before ("If only I hadn't knocked back that last Stinger").

A morbid stratagem, in surprisingly wide use, is to whisper hoarsely, "That chemo sure takes a lot out of you."

Once you've announced your Excuse for Poor Performance, you can set about to play briskly, having stripped your opponent of any pride he might have taken in beating you. Should you score an upset victory, he'll have no choice but to slink away in humiliation.

Tennis Etiquette

Tennis etiquette is an important part of the game. When your opponent is preparing to serve, it's bad form to try to throw him off with cheap distractions ("Hold it right there, I see a gnat on your shoulder").

When the ball drops close to the line in the opposite court, it's your opponent's call as to whether it's in or out, and his judgment should be accepted graciously. Try not to be spiteful if you disagree with him ("Go ahead and *take* the point. Some of us aren't that desperate").

As a Slightly Older Guy, you'll be expected to behave decently in either victory or defeat. After a loss, you don't want to be seen skulking away, muttering dark threats of revenge. And should you win the match, there's no need for you to leap over the net in triumph, clap your opponent on the back, and say, "It could have gone either way." Nor is it attractive to follow the losing player into the locker room with a satisfied smirk. A simple handshake will suffice, or at most a sly wink, indicating that, after all, you *did* win the match.

Some Other Considerations

EQUIPMENT

Care should be taken in the selection of equipment, but with an understanding that eye-catching footwear and a racket that's been endorsed by Ivan Lendl are no substitutes for clean ground strokes. Courtesy requires, too, that you show up before each match with a new can of balls. Repeatedly saying "We might as well use yours" will quickly identify you as a cheapskate. And being spotted rooting around in the shrubbery for used balls will only cause talk among the other players.

PREPARATION

Stretching out before a match is a sound idea, as is tossing back an aspirin or two as a means of fending off that scourge of all tennis enthusiasts, the dreaded hamstring pull. Worse than the injury itself is the player who'll stand over your crumpled form and deliver a diagnosis: "I believe you've popped your hammy."

A Little Respect

Be kind to your opponent. If he insists on winning every point, let him go ahead and do so. As a Slightly Older Guy, you've at least theoretically moved beyond such banal concerns as winning or losing. You have the advantage of knowing that the results of your match are not going to be splashed all over *The New York Times,* pushing assaults on Bosnia to the back pages. And there's no need to bear a grudge against a victorious opponent. As a younger man, you might have thought to yourself, "The little shit is going to tell everyone he beat me." With the mantle of wisdom on your shoulders, you can now sit back philosophically and say to yourself, "So *what* if the little shit tells everyone he beat me."

So go out there on the court, Slightly Older Guy, while there's still time and you're still able. You'll experience a sense of confidence and well-being, not overnight necessarily, but eventually, if you can just hang on long enough.

Some Other Roads
to Fitness

As a Slightly Older Guy, you're no doubt worried
sick about not getting enough exercise—but this is not that
bad. There is some evidence that worry itself, particularly
among members of the Jewish faith,* can result in a lean
and haggard look that often passes for fitness.

So don't worry about worrying.

Here are some other notions.

WALKING

If running, and even jogging, has become a strain, you might
want to give some thought to walking. Call it "speed-walk-
ing" if it makes you feel better. Walking is obviously easier
on the increasingly fragile knees, and there are circulatory
benefits as well, particularly if the arms are swung out smartly,
and away from the body, in the fascist style. (Don't overdo
this or you'll set off counterdemonstrations by peace groups.)

WALKING AND RUNNING

There's no law that says you can't do both. That is, run a
bit, walk when you get tired, then break into a run when

*Those who've been expecting "Slightly Older Goy" jokes are ad-
vised to look elsewhere.

you've rested up. Tell yourself that you're doing "wind sprints."

Only the purists will object to this hybrid workout. ("Now see here. I've been watching you. Either walk or run, damnit.")

BIKING

Hazardous, of course, if you're dodging in and out of city traffic, but worth considering if you can get out to the country-side. You'll have to wear one of those ridiculous mushroom-shaped helmets that are mandatory in many areas. Factor in the fresh air, the scenery—and it's still excruciatingly bor-ing. Try mixing it in with another more purposeful activ-ity—such as delivering newspapers.

WORKOUT TAPES

An excellent means of getting off the ground in the morn-ing. Be careful not to get caught up in Cindy Crawford's gyrations and forget to exercise.

AEROBICS

Best performed in classes, which are obviously a great place to meet women. Before dating a classmate, make sure you've seen her at least once when she's not in spandex.

TREADMILLS, STAIRMASTERS

Here again, an activity that's stultifyingly dull. If you're determined to get on one of these machines, be sure to have some reading material. See to it that it's not too intriguing or you'll forget to get off.

This is an excellent way to get through Proust.

*   *   *

Take your exercise where and when you can. Leaping enthusiastically to your feet during exciting moments of a ball game can make for a nice little workout. Watching tennis matches from center court has been known to reduce neck fat.

"The Doctor Will See You Now"

If you're a representative Slightly Older Guy, you'll probably insist on being in the pink of condition before you see a doctor—and, of course, you'll be missing the point. The idea is not to impress the doctor with your health. If you show up when you're brimming over with vitality, there's very little he can do for you other than clap you on the shoulder and tell you to keep up the good work, which is hardly worth the money. So visit the doctor when there's something wrong with you. And don't worry about alarming him. No matter what you've come up with, the chances are he's run across a case or two of it before, perhaps in the tropics.

Credible Credentials

Under the new health-care reform, it's unlikely you'll get to see a doctor you want to be in the same room with, much less be treated by. But assuming you have a say in the matter, choose one who is not only competent but who is certified to practice medicine—and not just in the Andaman Islands. And if he's not affiliated with a reputable hospital, don't accept his explanation that he's been misunderstood—or that his only crime was that he tried too hard. Insist that he have a license.

Your best bet is to consult a doctor who is roughly your age and who won't be baffled by your condition.

If you're sitting on the examining table and you say, "Bet you've never seen anything like *this* before," the answer you want to hear is: "No, no. I've had it myself for years."

Older doctors tend to be conservative and won't recommend radical procedures when you stub your toe. But if you see one, make sure to inquire about *his* health. It can be discomforting to have a doctor die in your arms.

Women in Medicine

It's possible you've been shying away from doctors of the opposite sex because they're constructed differently and will be in the dark as to how your body functions. This is misguided. A female doctor can be counted on to have done her homework. To at least have a passing acquaintance with your anatomy is part of her job.

Ultimately, what you want is a doctor who shows up now and then and isn't away snorkeling when you feel your life is slipping away.

Just Testing

Preventive medicine is much in vogue and requires that you schedule an annual checkup (it can be tied in with the yearly inspection of your car). Some people see this as a needless expense, but one justification of the cost is that doctors are always going to find something wrong with you that will be covered, at least in part, by your medical insurance. You can make that a condition of the checkup if you like.

Tests will generally be ordered up, and they can be unnerving, although it isn't the tests themselves so much as waiting for the results that accounts for a considerable number of fatalities in America. Many a Slightly Older Guy has for his epitaph: "I'm still waiting for my test results." And when a report finally does roll in, there's a strong chance

you'll get someone else's results, which may not always be a
bad thing.

A favorite of many is the stress test, which amounts to
not much more than a bracing little workout. There are
Slightly Older Guys who sign up for the test as a substitute
for jogging. Less appealing are CAT scans and MRI tests,
which can be terrifying because of all the mysterious equipment. It's best to start with the familiar thermometer and
blood pressure cuffs. As for the surrender of your body flu-
ids, do it as graciously as possible.

There Goes the Arm

When it's finally sunk in that you're an official Slightly
Older Guy, you may find yourself overreacting to the most
trivial of symptoms. A slight swelling of the elbow and you'll
be ready to say goodbye to your arm. At the onset of postnasal drip, you'll find yourself dashing off a living will.

Even a clean bill of health won't appease you. If your
doctor says you're in reasonably good health, don't panic and
cry out, "What do you mean by 'reasonably'?" Of course, a
slight touch of hypochondria is to be expected. Yet even in
the case of the most robust Slightly Older Guy, a time will
come when something really *has* gone amiss, which is why
you'll find it useful to live near a hospital.

Pop in and say hello to the admitting personnel at the
emergency room so they know you're friendly and won't be
carrying an assault rifle if you're ever carted in. And if you
have some spare time, work as a volunteer, not only to help
the unfortunate but to build up some goodwill in case you
ever need to be resuscitated. Additionally, see if you can get
a Fast-Track card so that if you pound a nail into your palm,
you can be whisked right through and won't have to spend
a weekend filling out forms.

Get in and out of these places as fast as possible. If you're
ever forced actually to stay in a hospital, make sure that you

have an escape plan worked out, so that you can slip away
in case anyone tries to do something to you.

Do-It-Yourself Medications

Overall, you'll want to stay as far away as you can from
hospitals and doctors; once you get involved with them,
there's no telling where it can lead. When something's not
quite right, very often the best treatment is to pop an aspirin and take a nap. Aspirin is every bit the wonder drug it's
cracked up to be, although a great deal of pressure has been
put on it—and you can't, for example, expect it to function
as a knee replacement.

Don't look down at home remedies. Chicken soup, for
example, has proven healing powers provided the chickens
were raised in a good barn. Cranberry juice is excellent for
the urinary tract, although it may keep your lips in a pucker.
Mustard is effective in clearing out the sinus passages, and
Grey Poupon will clear them out permanently. For ward-
ing off colds, there's always a clove of garlic, which is even
more effective when taken with veal marsala.

If It's Long Life You're After

Health, it will become increasingly clear, is more important than stocks and bonds, even when they're in medical
supplies. And illness is a great equalizer. If disaster strikes,
your lofty status isn't going to do you much good. When
your doctor tells you you're a very sick man, don't say, "There
must be some mistake. I'm the assistant merchandising director of Allied Chemical." You're just not going to get any
points for that. If the Sultan of Bahrain comes down with
Kunstler's syndrome, he's in the same boat as the poor man
who holds the door for him, although it's true that he can
send for Kunstler and see how *he* deals with it.

Much of what happens is out of your hands. If Schreiber's knee has been in the family for years, there's a chance you'll get a dose of it, and the best you can do is hold the line at one knee. It's fairly clear that common sense and not panic is the key to longevity. Stay out of the rain, don't let anyone sneeze at you, and remember that constant worry about your health is the quickest path to the grave. Let someone else worry about it. Marry a nurse. And above all, keep busy. The Slightly Older Guy who is always dashing off to seminars doesn't have *time* to get sick. And if you do come down with something, remember, there are worse things—such as an IRS audit.

Two Sinful Pursuits

SMOKING

Although a great many Slightly Older Guys have given up cigarettes, still others continue to puff away with abandon. Some do so in morbid defiance of death, considering each inhalation a little attention-getting challenge to their mortality. Others take a Clintonesque stance, saying they don't inhale, hoping against hope that the tobacco companies are right and that smoking is just a harmless and amusing pastime. The Slightly Older Guy, too, might claim that he came of age at a time when film stars couldn't wait to finish their (offstage) lovemaking so they could blow clouds of smoke at each other. Or he'll remind you that it was impossible to be taken seriously as a person of worldly substance unless your eyes were pained and squinted and there was a cigarette dangling from your lips.

Dollars and Sense

"I've tried everything and I can't stop," the Slightly Older Guy might say in frustration. "I guess I'm just a smoker to the end."

Not necessarily. There's always the appeal of economic self-interest—which is generally the cause of wars, revolutions, and most human behavior. Try calculating the amount of money you've spent on cigarettes over the last year—or over the past decade, for that matter—and you might find

the figure alarming. There are Slightly Older Guys who believe they've come into a mysterious financial windfall, with coins spilling out of their pockets, before they realize their good fortune began the day they gave up smoking.

The Old Dazzle

When the above tactic doesn't work, you might, in a last-ditch effort to lose the habit, try appealing to your vanity.

There's an obligation to report here—with some reluctance—that the teeth begin to yellow a bit in the natural aging process. This, combined with smoking, can result in a gray and grungy look about the mouth, desirable perhaps in the resident poet at Swarthmore but unappetizing in the case of the average Slightly Older Guy.

The good news here is that there is a new process* that, in roughly two weeks' time, can whiten your teeth, add some sparkle to them, and virtually restore the smile you had in your college yearbook photo. The bad news is that this remarkable process will reverse itself if you continue to smoke.

So the choice is yours. Do you return to the habit that secretly made you cringe with embarrassment and has obviously put you on a downhill slide? Or do you go forth with the killer smile that once impressed cheerleaders and never failed to cause a stir at parties? Slightly Older Guys who've chosen the latter option report having a new bounce in their step—and are somewhat puzzled about why they ever smoked in the first place.

DRINKING

As a Slightly Older Guy, you might consider yourself a moderate drinker, a fellow who knocks back a cocktail or two in order to sharpen your appetite and make the world

*Night White.

seem a bit more agreeable. And you've no doubt been heart-
ened by the medical finding that drinking, when held in
check, helps guarantee a long and robust life.

"That's me, all right," you might point out. "I'll have one
or two to steel myself for Peter Jennings and the evening
news. After that, you can't sell me a drink."

No one says you have to give up this pleasurable activity.
But if your evenings have been passing by in a blur and you
can vaguely recall any of the following situations, it may be
that you're no longer, strictly speaking, just a moderate
drinker:

- You make nightly calls to the White House, de-
  manding an invasion of Canada.
- You can't remember your phone number.
- Several mornings a week, you wake up on lawns.

Sound familiar? Then you might want to have a look at
what it is—and how much of it—you've been drinking. Let's
face it, a pint-sized tumbler of Old Rotgut amounts to more
than a harmless little pick-me-up. And the chances are you
don't even recollect all the brandy and wine that followed.
As a Slightly Older Guy, your memory has already taken a
pounding. Give it a break.

When you're a Slightly Older Guy, you'll also discover
that, through some quirk of body chemistry, one drink now
does the work of four. Unfortunately, the same principle
holds true for hangovers, which can no longer be waved off
with a nap and a cup of coffee. You've got to account for a
full day or two before you're back on your feet—which are
not all that steady to begin with.

Part Three

Affairs of
the Heart

A Circle of Friends

From the day it sinks in that you are, indeed, a Slightly Older Guy, it's essential that you surround yourself with a supportive group of old friends. Rounding them up may not be as easy as you might think. Some, you'll find, are being maintained on Prozac and are afraid to leave the house. Others will have moved to remote parts of the globe, such as Kansas City. A few may want to have nothing more to do with you. If any remain, it's important to treasure them and to forgive them their minor transgressions. If a friend occasionally cries out, "You've always been a selfish bastard," take him aside, humor him gently, and try to put his outbursts in perspective. Maybe there's some truth to the charge. Assure him that in the future you'll go out of your way not to be a selfish bastard. If he continues to denounce you at large public gatherings, you have every right to question his loyalty.

The Slightly Older Guy who feels that he's friendless and alone may have a wide variety of opportunities staring him in the face and not realize it.

Some examples:

THE ENDODONTIST

Don't disqualify your endodontist as a potential friend just because he's spent years plugging up your root canals. Without his mask, and away from his gas delivery system, he may come off as an entirely different person.

Invite him on a fishing trip. Once you've fried your catch and are lying beneath the stars, sound him out on his hopes and fears and dreams, not just for a better America but for the future of root canal work. He may turn out to be a wonderful new friend. In this same spirit, you might want to take a fresh look at your accountant. Invite him to a concert. If the evening doesn't work out, you can always write it off.

THE OPPOSITE SEX

It may be that you haven't been paying sufficient attention to women in the context of friendship. You may not know it, but women are the best confidantes and will guard your secrets from all but their closest girlfriends. Then, too, they can be counted on to give you the very latest information on What Women Want. And the fact that a female friend will outlive you by an average of seven years means she'll be around to speak highly of you when you're gone.

And remember: in forging friendships with women, try to keep sex out of it unless it's absolutely necessary. But if sex does work its way in, you may find yourself with that most remarkable of all combinations—a lover *and* a friend.

MAN'S BEST FRIEND

Dogs are completely nonjudgmental, and that quality alone makes them the most loyal of companions. If you're forced to commit an ax murder in your dog's presence, he'll turn the other way, as long as he's fed on time. Remember, however, that friendship with a dog does have its limits. You may be able to share your innermost thoughts and feelings with a schnauzer, but you can't expect him to reciprocate.

FAIR-WEATHER FRIENDS

If you find yourself a little short of friends, it may be that you've set your standards too high.

"Sven will never make *my* list," you might say snappishly. "He's a fair-weather friend."

Perhaps that's true, but at least Sven is around in fair weather. Which is more than you can say for your enemies. Not every friend can be counted on to nurse you back to health when you come down with a cold. Or lend you his Harley-Davidson. And it's only the rare friend who'll rush over with a howitzer when you're having a boundary dispute with your neighbor.

Lighten up. Don't insist that your friends be of the highest moral fiber. Many a fascinating evening has been spent with an acquaintance who's under indictment and has to wear electronic leg irons.

OLDER FRIENDS

To the extent that they exist, try to cultivate a circle of friends who are even older than you are. Their concerns may be a little downbeat—Successful Bypasses, Interactive Walkers, the Joy of Dying in Your Sleep—but they'll provide you with some idea of what's in your not-so-distant future. As the youngest member of such a group, your only responsibility will be to sit back and listen, murmuring an occasional "That was way before my time." You'll come away feeling like a pup and looking, by comparison, like a Slightly Younger Guy.

WIVES

Fortunate is the Slightly Older Guy who can count his wife as a friend.

"I don't need anyone else," you might declare, perhaps with a little smugness. "Not when I have Megan at my side." It's important to be honest here. Megan may be a wonderful woman, but has she always been at your side? What about the time when the cucumber slice was stuck in your throat and Megan wouldn't stop watching *All My Children*? Wasn't it the FedEx man who administered the Heimlich maneuver?

No disrespect for Megan, but why saddle her with the responsibilities of friendship? She has enough trouble being a wife.

DON'T BE A STRANGER

The rules of friendship are far from rigid, but you do have to make contact once in a while.

"Carl and I don't *have* to speak," you might say in rebuttal. "Our friendship is beyond that."

That may be true, but do you have to let thirty years go by before calling him? Carl might be an entirely different person now. Maybe he's had a sex change. There might not even *be* a Carl anymore. So pick up the phone. And don't start wondering why he hasn't called you. He may not have *heard* about your gallbladder. Or maybe he lost your number. Isn't it possible that Carl has fallen on hard times and can't afford a long-distance call?

Life's too short—just give the man a ring.

Ingredients of Friendship

- A good friend will care about your well-being. Pinching at your hip fat and saying, "Gained a few pounds there, haven't we, fella?" is not a genuine display of concern.
- The stalwart friend can be counted on to show up at important milestones in your life, ranging from birthday parties to jury trials for insider trading.

- A good friend will have a eulogy prepared well in advance of your funeral—as you'll no doubt have one on hand for his. (It's not useful to speculate morbidly on who'll get to deliver his speech first.)
- Wealth should not be held against a friend as long as he's prepared to hand some of it over now and then. Nor should fame stand in the way of camaraderie. The Slightly Older Guy, with a secure sense of himself, will think nothing of inviting Kevin Costner into his inner circle.

A Great Friend

Wives may come and go, children leave home, but a true friend is in it for the long haul. Short of being thrown out of the house, he'll remain at your side until the closing curtain. And losing a friend is a grave matter indeed, not to be put in the same category as a lost sweater. A true friendship takes years to develop. You can't spend a night on the town with a Florida real estate speculator you met at a bar and expect him to take the place of Doodles McKenzie, whom you've known since grade school.

The ideal friend will say little, chuckle amiably at familiar anecdotes, and not repeat attacks on your character that he's overheard in the locker room of your club. He'll be responsive to your changing moods. You may have been relying on one friend for discussions of William Gaddis novels and another for company at topless mud-wrestling events, but the ideal friend will happily accommodate both tastes.

As a Slightly Older Guy, you may decide one night to stop worrying about friends; your own company is all you'll ever need. Having arrived at that conclusion, simply take yourself to a hockey game. Eventually, however, you'll discover that there is no substitute for a real friend—ideally one who's on the homely side and can always be counted on to be in worse shape than you are.

Divorce—and the Ex-Wife

As a Slightly Older Guy, there's a good chance you've been divorced and have an ex-wife or two floating about somewhere. This is not a particularly pleasant situation to contemplate. An ex-wife conjures up thoughts of What Might Have Been, the sheer waste of it, the monstrous legal fees that could so easily have been diverted to other causes and pastimes, such as the pursuit of your present wife. And the financial pain that followed your divorce. Not that she's to blame. No one doubts her need for support. But once her ostrich farm began to thrive, surely she could have returned an alimony payment or two. Just as a token of gratitude.

As it happens, there's no such thing as divorce. You may have a legal document that *says* you've been set free, but the memories—bittersweet if you're lucky—continue to form a bond. If there are children in the picture, you're bound to be flung together, at a son's engagement, a daughter's folk-singing debut. Years may have passed, but there's always one more document to be signed, and there continue to be grounds for a case, however weak, of spousal abuse. You may have already formulated your defense: "Hey, listen, *I'm* not the one who hired a hit man."

A Game Plan

What's to be done about it? As little as possible. It's probably better to let sleeping dogs lie. Plan a sociable lunch if you like, but keep it at the planning stage. If you go forward with the idea, a single unfortunate reference will inevitably cause voices to be raised and drinks flung in your face. It's possible to remain in civilized touch with an ex-wife, but only in the world of Noël Coward.

Approach all phone calls warily. They'll start off pleasantly enough, but there's always going to be a dark subtext, generally a costly one. Rare is the ex-wife who calls just to see how you're getting along.

The key to amiable coexistence on the same planet is to stay out of her life—and hope she stays out of yours. Don't even wonder what she's up to. With luck, she will have remarried. If she's remained unattached, resist the impulse to send a friend out there to court her. She didn't care for you. Why would she like him?

Perhaps she was your first love, but that may as well have been in Precambrian times. Think of the experience as having helped make you a seasoned Slightly Older Guy.

Your ex-wife knew you when you thought nothing of punching out headwaiters and taking naps on highway dividers with a bottle of Jack Daniel's as a pillow. There's no need for her to know how civilized you've become.

Wish your ex-wife well. Tell her you hope that she lives to be one hundred and has a rich, fulfilling life in Winnipeg.

The Slightly Older Wife

Fortunate is the Slightly Older Guy who has somehow managed to stay married—even though he now has a Slightly Older Wife.

There are great advantages to being in this situation. Companionship, shared experiences, an acceptance of your many eccentricities, the willingness to overlook snores and gargling sounds that might prove unappealing to a younger mate. Someone to assist you if you've slipped on an anchovy. Communication in shorthand, especially in the bedroom, where a single code word such as *scissors* or *fleaflicker* is all that's required in assuming a favored intimate position.

With a Slightly Older Wife as a companion, there's no need to fill up silences with idle chitchat.

With luck, you may not have to talk at all.

Words of Caution

Along with the comforts of having a Slightly Older Wife, there are also areas of great sensitivity that are best not ignored.

Here are some advisories:

- Endearments such as "sweet old thing" and "good old gal," no matter how well intentioned, are bound to be taken in the wrong spirit—and should be held to a minimum.

- If a few gray hairs show up on your Slightly Older Wife's head, don't be the first to point them out ("Aha, what have we here?"). The chances are she's already spotted them. Then, too, humming "The Old Gray Mare" is not reassuring.
- Don't try to justify the hiring of an attractive young assistant by pointing to her exceptional background and the dent she's going to put in your workload. Hire a plain-looking young woman and hope there are hidden fires burning within her.
- Pay strict attention to birthdays and anniversaries, even if this requires nailing up poster-sized reminders in your office. Make sure that gifts are thought out carefully and are personal in nature. Black & Decker tool kits will not be appreciated. In this area, a sudden, unannounced gift, for no particular purpose, will put you in good standing for some time to come—and won't necessarily indicate that you've started having an affair.
- If your Slightly Older Wife lies about her age, don't correct the error. Let it slide. That'll make her less likely to correct you when you tell a friend, "Oh, I only put on about four or five pounds."
- When a Slightly Older Wife parades in with an outrageous new hairstyle—and you hadn't noticed anything wrong with the old one—tell her she reminds you of a young Greta Garbo.
- Your sex life may have become subdued and even "cozy," but there's no need to point this out at every turn. Should a Slightly Older Wife exhibit a sudden burst of sexuality, rein in your surprise ("What's gotten into you?") and try to keep up with her.
- Don't sulk if her career has blazed on ahead of yours. Count your blessings, tidy up the house, and hope she likes what you've fixed for dinner.
- Include her in your vacation plans. The idea of

tooling around Amsterdam unencumbered may
seem appealing, but remember, you're a Slightly
Older Guy now, amorous adventures are few and
far between, and you'll probably end up sight-seeing
all by yourself.

Care, concern, respect—those are the watchwords. A
Slightly Older Wife has invested heavily in you, however
rashly. This has put her in the same boat as you, and after
all this time you might as well sail off into the sunset
together.

And Under No Circumstances

Never confess an adultery, no matter how long it's
been buried in the past. In a Ferenc Molnár story, a
ninety-year-old man tells his ninety-year-old wife of
an affair he had with her friend, fifty years back. With
her two remaining teeth, she bites off the tip of his
nose.

The Slightly Older Guy and His Kids

Here are some thoughts for the Slightly Older Guy about his children:

- Don't be disappointed if your son doesn't follow in your footsteps. Grit your teeth and try to be encouraging. At some later date, he may decide to give up the tattoo parlor and join you in dentistry.
- It's not a betrayal if a son or daughter doesn't share your taste in music. Not all teenagers are drawn to Perry Como.
- Even if you suspect that a son or daughter isn't really yours, don't banish the kid from your affections. It's possible to learn to love a child who is growing up to closely resemble your accountant.
- If your mature son decides to move out of the house, don't grab him by the lapels and beg him to stay. Say goodbye graciously and enjoy the free time you have until he moves back.
- Child-rearing is expensive, and it's naïve to think you'll get back every penny of your investment. Remember, you spent all that money out of love. If a child succeeds in the world and wants to reward you with a personal Gulfstream jet, grab it before he changes his mind and gives it to his mother.

- It's natural to continue to think of sons and daughters as your kids, even when they're heading up multinational conglomerates. But try to draw the line at age forty.
- Sex continues to be a delicate area in the rearing of children. Give it a great deal of thought before turning the whole business over to your wife. (Then when your kids start having kids, you can safely assume they've got the hang of it.)
- If your daughter shows up with a potential mate who's clearly not the rocket scientist you had in mind, hide your feelings and try to be a good sport about it. Keep in mind that your future father-in-law didn't exactly faint with delight when you appeared on the scene.
- Inevitably, your Slightly Older Kid is going to have a child of his own. He'll generally announce the event with a chilling midnight call: "Guess what? I'm presenting you with a grandchild." When someone addresses you as "Grandpa," you'll probably be unamused at first, whipping your head around and saying, "I beg your pardon . . ." But Cary Grant got used to it. You can, too. At the extreme, you might even wind up with one of those bumper stickers that says defiantly:

"Grandparent—and proud of it." And there's no question you'll grow to love the new member of the team, racing out to Minnesota once a month to make sure he's getting his share of pony rides.

Dating—and the Eleventh-Hour Romance

With the clock ticking at a maddening pace, the Slightly Older Guy who has been triumphant as a bachelor may suddenly panic at the thought of finding himself stranded in the late innings with no comforting hand to see him through. There are practical matters to consider. What if he falls down the stairs in the middle of the night and there's no one standing by to cart him off to the hospital? Or does he really want to tour the Greek islands as a solitary passenger, staring out at the Aegean, with no one to share his reflections on antiquity?

If you find yourself in this position—or if you're a Slightly Older Guy who is newly divorced—you may be a bit shaky when it comes to the rituals of romance. But there's no reason to rush off an application for a mail-order bride. Nor trust your fate to a computer dating service. Available women can be found close to home and in the most mundane of settings. The supermarket, for example, is generally teeming with prospects. An amusing remark at the checkout counter to an attractive fellow shopper can lead to the most rewarding of liaisons ("I see we're both Boar's Head ham enthusiasts").

The post office, too, is brimming with possibilities. And here again, a clever offhand comment ("How about those new Elvis commemoratives!") may very well yield romantic dividends.

Some Interesting Candidates

Laundromats are generally filled with comely young Irish wenches, just in from County Cork and looking for a sponsor, ideally a Slightly Older Guy with a spare room. Bookstores, too, have become a magnet for serious-minded women with romance on their agenda. Particularly appealing are those clustered around the Isak Dinesen shelves. And there's no need to turn your nose up at topless dancers, assuming that a supple and exposed body is a sign of meager intelligence. By day, a surprising number are enrolled at the NYU film school. Others are hard at work on Willa Cather theses. In fact, it's not uncommon to run across a stripper who's a wizard at molecular biology.

Vintage Material

The Slightly Older Guy who has spent most of his years swinishly dating younger women will discover an entirely new world when he hooks up with a contemporary. Shared recollections of John Foster Dulles and Nelson Eddy are certain to be enlivening. Proceeding more boldly in this direction, you might even consider taking up with a woman who is considerably older than you are. If you decide to head this way, try for a grande dame type who's spent a great deal of her time in Paris and palled around with Anaïs Nin.

An Assortment of Other Choices

A good many Slightly Older Guys have begun to target nurses, not only for their romantic potential but as a means of setting up an in-house alternative to the Clinton health plan. There's no need to stalk the corridors of hospitals in search of prospects, but if you happen to be paying a deathbed visit to an old colleague, there's no harm in taking a good look at the nurse who's seeing him through—and don't forget to take note of the quality of her work.

Actresses, as is commonly known, are cheerful and attractive companions, but they're away on location a good deal of the time, making them vulnerable to affairs with Keanu Reeves. Particularly interesting are Women Who Tag Along at Dinner Parties. Many are wounded creatures, haunted and star-crossed. Others are fresh and spirited and open to challenge. In any case, there's something captivating about a tagalong. You'll find yourself wanting to see to it that she never has to tag along again.

In casting about for a romantic teammate, try not to be taken in by a single characteristic—a passing resemblance to Deborah Norville, for example, or an imitation of Julio Iglesias doing bird calls, which is bound to pale on repetition. And don't be taken in by a British accent, which can make the most routine comment sound Shakespearean. "I'll just pop into the loo" sounds eloquent on the lips of a rascal just in from Sheffield, but doesn't really add up to much when its content is examined closely.

A Word of Caution

Be wary of women who toss their hair a lot. It's difficult to build something lasting on this one attribute. And remember that chronic hair-tossing can lead to serious neck injury.

The Opening Gambit

"All right, all right," you say. "I'll take your word for it. Maybe there are women all over the place. So what if I spot one? How do I get the thing started?"

For openers, there's no need to lie about your age. On the other hand, you don't have to be overly forthright about it,

either ("I'm Todd Mullins and guess what—I'm fifty-two").
Nor do you want to come on too forcefully by boasting about
your accomplishments. Hold off for a bit before announc-
ing that you're head of the neighborhood improvement
association.

Salt in your credits slowly and gracefully. Do the same
with your marital history. You want to avoid kicking off a
new friendship with the story of your two divorces and the
many shortcomings of your former wives.

Very often, the best opening remark is simple and direct.
"How are you tonight?" is a perfectly acceptable ice-
breaker—unless, of course, it's daytime.

Your Next Move

Fortunate is the Slightly Older Guy who has a romance
that's briskly under way. But he'll soon have to make up his
mind as to whether he wants to Live Together with his new
companion—or push ahead to what, in many cases, will be
a second or even third try at marriage. The former is a precarious arrangement; since either partner is free to light out
at a moment's notice, it involves a certain amount of walking on eggs. As to the more secure alternative, the Slightly
Older Guy who's been round the marital horn before will
want to proceed with particular caution. With time in short
supply, the last thing he needs for his end game is another
bitter face-off in divorce court—this time with Raoul Felder.

There is no need to tick off the many criticisms that have
been directed at marriage. We all know what they are, and
of course, confinement generally heads the list. Yet in the
teeth of this, there are Slightly Older Guys who insist it's
marriage that's always afforded them the greatest degree of
freedom.

"I'm so free that I don't *have* to have affairs."

If this is freedom, then so be it.

The Swan-Song Affair

In quite another situation is the Slightly Older Guy who's been comfortably married for a decade or so but feels there's something missing in his life.

"It's not Tanya," he might say. "Tanya's great and I guess I love her. She's my best friend and we get on decently enough in bed. And yet . . ."

And yet: the two plaintive words that generally signal a yearning for an Eleventh-Hour Romance—and the despondent feeling that the Slightly Older Guy is fated not to experience one. Never again the stolen kiss in a taxi, the anxious phone call, the inevitable theme song, the dizziness, the anticipation, the damp and sultry consummation on a hot night in August in the empty city.

"How I'd love to have another one of those," the Slightly Older Guy might lament. "And if I can't, I might as well pack it in."

If these are your true feelings, there's no point in casting about aimlessly for a love affair. But inevitably, in the course of a normal life, one is bound to creep up on you with little warning. A handshake, the merest glance, and there it is, having come into being in mystery and silence, like a virus.

The question then becomes one of whether to go forward in madness, ignoring Tanya's years of devotion and all that you've built together in Armonk. And this is not to mention little Tanya. Do you turn your back on her as well?

Don't delude yourself by thinking that you can keep any of this from the instinctively brilliant Tanya herself. She's bound to guess the instant you present her with the guilt-scented bouquet ("You're seeing another woman, aren't you? Why, Budd, why?").

The wisest move at this point—as if wisdom has anything to do with it—is to do and say as little as possible, and to retreat for a brief period from Tanya as well as the object of your infatuation. If you can manage it, spend a week alone, perhaps on an Indian reservation, allowing your passions to cool—and assuring Tanya with repeated phone calls that you're spending all your time placing bets on Keno. At the end of your trip, you may well decide to plunge ahead and tear your life to shreds by starting what's left of it anew with your fresh discovery.

But remember, it's late in the day, and there's always the risk of botching the whole business and eventually ending up with neither Tanya nor her replacement in a rooming house in Santa Monica, alone with your liver spots. The saner course is to accept your loss and remain with Tanya—if she'll take you back.

"I've had it with love," you might declare if Tanya has washed her hands of you, wondering if the sentiment might not catch fire as a country-western lyric.

And then, just as you've resigned yourself to a joyless, loveless, humdrum existence, you might attend a function one night and catch a glimpse across the buffet table of a slender form, an intriguing profile, a heartbreaking cascade of silken hair, all of it capped off by a throaty and engaging laugh.

"Oh my God," you think, caught off guard, reeling. "Who *is* she? I've got to meet her."

Then she turns—and it's Tanya.

A Young Wife

If you're an unattached Slightly Older Guy, you may have toyed with the idea of taking a young wife. Assuming there's one available, you'll find that there are many attractive features to this option. Heads will turn when you enter restaurants, roués will lift their glasses in admiration, and only on occasion will some spoilsport be overheard whispering, "What on God's earth is she doing with him?"

There will be an assumption that you're quite a virile fellow and that power and money are yours as well, when in actuality you may have a total of four hundred dollars in the bank.

Using your young wife as a beard, you'll be able to slip into Lemonheads concerts.

Challenged to keep up with a youthful bride, you'll find yourself performing feats of strength you thought were beyond you—such as lifting couches and, in a more playful vein, lifting your young wife as well.

At nightclubs, she'll drag you out onto the dance floor and encourage you to gyrate wildly with the music. And if you don't keep up, you'll be bumped off the floor, the sound of "Gramps" echoing in your ears.

Some Other Perks

Along with a young wife will come a whole group of young friends, and it's entirely possible that several may ask to hide out in your apartment for a few months. A completely new family will come along as part of the package, too, and you can't assume that all will be the salt of the earth. Some time may have to be set aside for visiting an aunt or two in institutions.

A young wife will see you as a mentor and will listen attentively as you fill her in on the defense of Stalingrad. All your stories will be fresh to her ("Tell me one more time about the night you met Senator Al D'Amato at a fundraiser"), and you will be surprised to find that you tell them with a new verve.

As a young person, she probably hasn't seen all that much of the world, and you can look forward to her high excitement when she's taken to Manhattan and shown the Chrysler Building.

No request for sexual pleasure will be denied, even when you wish it would be. (For an expansion of this theme, see section on "Sex and the Slightly Older Guy.") You may, on occasion, long for the company of someone who remembers Ed Meese, but there are treats in store that will easily compensate for this minor void in your life. For example, a young wife will expose you to an entirely new approach to the English language ("Like don't you think this place is like totally cool?").

A Few Drawbacks

There's no question that a young wife will lift your spirits, but there are some disadvantages to the arrangement that must be considered. For all of her tender years, she may require extensive dental work. And there may have been a brief earlier marriage that somehow slipped her mind—to someone named "Whalebone" who keeps showing up and asking for money to tide him over until he lands another bartender job.

Coming as she does from a more recent generation, a young wife will tend to be more concerned about the planet than you are and could very well hold you personally responsible for the California water shortage. You may find she has stationed herself outside the bathroom door to time your showers and listen for extra flushes. In fact, if you've been counting on a double income, you may be unpleasantly surprised to learn that she's taken on an unpaid job with Friends of the Ozone Layer.

As a Slightly Older Guy, your taste in dining will no doubt have taken on some sophistication, and here, too, there can be trouble. With little interest in this pleasurable activity, a young wife may be puzzled by your lack of enthusiasm as she sets before you for dinner a Coke and a platter of onion rings. With your own digestive system becoming increasingly shaky, you'll wonder how one person can polish off all those chimichangas and still look so good.

She'll need much more sleep than you do, and as a result you may not see much of her during the daytime. As to the evening hours, she'll no doubt be much more attached to television than you are—and you might find yourself competing with Letterman for her attention.

An Addition to the Team

Inevitably, a young wife will make it known that motherhood is her ultimate goal in life. This need will be communicated by a certain look in her eyes, a newfound interest in all things related to infants, or a sudden anguished Medealike cry in a crowded elevator: *"I want a baby!"*

After you've made your apologies to the other passengers and ushered her outside, it might be a good idea to take this need of hers seriously. It doesn't matter that you've already produced three or four guitar players and turned them loose on the world—she hasn't, and it is probably wise to indulge her.

However, you'll find there's more to it this time around than just muddling through a good part of the following year and showing up at the hospital with cigars. Expecting a child means signing on for Lamaze classes, and as the senior member of the group you'll probably be the one chosen to play the part of the vulva. Extensive instruction will follow on the timing of contractions. Although you've been described as a coach, you'll be expected to do more during the delivery than holler "Way to go, babe!" It's entirely possible your wife will be so zonked out during much of the procedure that *you're* the one who'll be asked questions such as "Shall we shoot for an epidural?" It's useful to have an intelligent response prepared—and not simply wave casually and tell the doctor, "It's your dime."

"It's a Girl"

You can expect your new family member to blend into the household without too much disruption for a while, but become more conspicuous as time rolls along. It is important to remember here that you're a Slightly Older Guy. If you've come up with another son, an invitation to "shoot a few hoops" may be enough to send you packing off for a new life in Central Europe.

A daughter is another matter. Once you've calmed down and stopped running joyously and idiotically through the streets, you'll want to establish some rules, the most important of which is: No Dating Until Forty. Then it's simply a matter of laying down weaponry to discourage prospective suitors and learning to say "No." This, as you might guess, is not an easy task. There have been isolated reports of fathers turning down a daughter's request, but none can be verified.

Through all of this, be sure not to neglect your wife, who's still young (although not as young as your daughter). Both

will need to be indulged, which can be expensive as you'll
notice when the monthly Gap bills come rolling in. Pets will
undoubtedly be added to the family mix, and they are costly
as well.

Nonetheless, you'll see such expenditures as a small price
to pay as you settle down in your new life: a Slightly Older
Guy with a young wife, a daughter, a Japanese temple dog,
several cats, and a macaw.

Part Four

Affairs
of the
Pocketbook

Some Small and Painless Economies

It's not unreasonable to think that after years of slaving away as a gazebo salesman, you'd have a little something in the bank to show for it. But that isn't always the case. Take a cold, hard look at your finances. After factoring in mortgage payments, credit card charges, outstanding loans, and a few old plumbing bills, it may turn out that you have a net worth of $164 in cash. Or maybe you're $164 in the red. In either case, it's never too late to economize, even if you're a Slightly Older Guy.

Here are some thoughts on how to do so.

FORGET BRAND-NAME PRODUCTS

There's very little difference between generic ketchup and the real thing. You'll note, too, that your dog is just as happy wolfing down biscuits that come in a box with a plain label. Just don't let him in on it. As for aspirin, a generic tablet will get rid of most of your headache, if not all of it. And you don't have to buy generic products in an alleyway from someone named Lightning. They're available in major retail outlets and are generally kept over on the side somewhere.

SCALE DOWN YOUR OPERATION

If your income has fallen from $100,000 a year to, say, $4,750, it may be time to reconsider whether you really need a bookkeeper, an accountant, a lawyer, and a public relations adviser. Why keep on paying a financial planner when there's nothing to plan? Take on some of these functions yourself. Call it downsizing if it makes you feel better. Apply the same theory to your living quarters. If you've been keeping up a twelve-room house for some weird romantic reason ("It's where I want to die"), think about the fact that maintaining a huge house is one of the leading causes of death. Consider getting a smaller place. You don't have to go to the other extreme and rent a broom closet in Toledo. Just get something comfortable.

STOP REACHING FOR THE CHECK

Let someone else pick up the tab for a change. If a woman offers to pay for your dinner, don't wrestle her to the ground in an attempt to pry the check away from her. Let her pay the damned thing. You'll not only save a few bucks, you'll also help her to consolidate her hard-fought gains over the last decade.

Should this new, tight-fisted style make you less popular, you can always find new friends at church socials.

SCALE BACK YOUR TIPPING

And be a bit more selective about it. It's one thing to tip the waiter, but do you have to tip the owner of the restaurant, too? And the head of the chain? Of course not. They're doing just fine.

"But what about Sinatra?" you might ask. "He throws around hundred-dollar bills, and look at all the respect *he* gets."

To begin with, you're not Sinatra. Can you sing "My Way" with half the emotion he puts into it? Are you being paid $100,000 a night by Caesars and getting a big round of applause as you're carted away after fainting onstage? Forget Sinatra. Just go about your business and do it your way.

LOOK FOR "GOING OUT OF BUSINESS" SALES

Don't howl with laughter when you see an "Everything Must Go" sign in a store window and assume it's just a come-on. Some stores really *do* go out of business, and when they do, they give away merchandise at virtually bargain prices. But before you make a purchase, check with the owner and make sure he's *really* destitute.

PUMP YOUR OWN GAS

If someone sees you doing it, it's not as if you've been caught in a bordello. Many outstanding Americans now pump their own gas and are just as embarrassed about it as you are. It's an excellent way to get some fresh air, save a little money, and strike back at the oil emirates.

DON'T AUTOMATICALLY PAY THE CHECK THAT'S HANDED TO YOU

Restaurants make mistakes. For all you know, you may have been accidentally charged for some stockbroker's focaccia. When you don't even like focaccia. So go over the check every once in a while.* The restaurant won't care. And the next time you come in, you'll get an excellent table, if they're not too crowded.

PAY YOUR BILLS ON TIME

Unless you attend seminars and are surrounded by support groups, there's no point in trying to break the credit card habit. Maybe gene replacement is a solution. Meanwhile, you

---

*And while you're at it, check your monthly bank statement carefully. Now and then banks like to extract a few thousand dollars from your account just to see if you're on your toes,

can take a stab at paying your bills when they come in and avoiding finance charges. Those charges are the main reason so many Americans live below the poverty line—and why we can't catch Japan.

DON'T BE MISLED BY PRICE TAGS

Very often, the price is just something the store owner slapped on there. A $10 backscratcher isn't necessarily more effective at getting at itches than the $3.50 variety. Merchants pay a lot of attention to snob appeal. If they can't get rid of a jar of old pimientos, for example, they'll very often double the price—then sit back and watch it fly out of the store. Buying the cheaper item doesn't necessarily mean you're a cheap S.O.G.

TAKE A LOOK AT *MODERN MATURITY*

It's disheartening to think about it, but there are some items of interest in this magazine. You don't have to look at it in public. Close the blinds, dim the lights, and pick up a copy. Skimming over the breakthroughs in denture fasteners, move as quickly as possible to the reduced bus fares and airline tickets. When you call the bus company or airlines directly, you can say you're calling for an older brother who's shy and clams up on the phone.

ELIMINATE CABLE TV

You may not be able to pull it off, but it's worth a try. Small groups out West have attempted it and so far haven't experienced any serious side effects. They take hikes, put on little skits at home, and have developed a new appreciation for CBS. On nights when they just can't take it anymore, they watch other people's cable with binoculars. Give it a try.

Stanch the Flow

Don't be desperate about any of this. No one is asking you to recycle old Valentine's Day cards or to take home little sugar packets from restaurants. That's not going to restore you to financial health. But is there any reason why you can't go through your pockets before you send your clothing off to the dry cleaner? Or every now and then check behind the sofa cushions? A small economy may seem like a financial Band-Aid, but what's wrong with a little stopper in the sink until you figure out a way to keep from going totally down the drain.

Tighten your belt a bit and you'll be better prepared for the long haul—or the short haul, as it might be.

The (Forcibly) Retired Slightly Older Guy (and Some Career Opportunities)

"Retire? Who, me? Live in one of those communities in Sarasota? Spend all my time on the phone lobbying Congress about Medicare? Reminding them, in a thin but surprisingly firm voice, how many of us there are out here? That's not me. That's not even *close* to me. You're forgetting I'm only a *Slightly* Older Guy."

That may be true, but when it comes to retirement you may not have much say in the matter. Today, corporate downsizers are asking Slightly Older Guys to pack it in when they've barely gotten out of the gate.

A Gracious Farewell

If you're put in this situation, it won't do any good to complain that you've hardly had time to decorate your office. Or to point out that the Japanese would never treat an employee so shabbily, which may be why, incidentally, they've gotten the jump on us. Accept the inevitable with a smile and try to wangle the best retirement package you can, one that includes more than a box of office supplies and some coffee filters. If you're offered a farewell party, don't snap back that you'd rather have the money. Show up at the festivities, and if you're asked to make a few remarks, pay your respects to your co-workers, even if they're all twenty years younger and you can't remember their names.

Reflect back nostalgically on your triumphs and defeats, expressing amazement that it all seemed to go by in a flash—which, unfortunately, it did. Work hard on this presentation. If it's really good, maybe they'll hire you back.

If that doesn't happen, clean out your office quickly and stay away for good. Don't drop around every few days to see if they miss you. Or charge in with the latest sales figures and say, "I told you this would happen."

Regroup

Take a breather at this point, a little time to get your house in order. If you're married, make sure your wife is working, your children have jobs—and see if you can find something for the dog to do. Let your friends in on the situation so they can get ready to lend you money.

Check your retirement plan. Most Slightly Older Guys don't have one, just a rough timetable of how long they can hold out before they start asking for help. If you have a pension plan, make sure you can get your hands on the money. A lot of these plans are terrific, but they never quite kick in—at least not when you need them. And don't be thrown if the fellow who runs the plan is under indictment and awaiting trial.

There's no reason to be embarrassed about your situation. You're not the only Slightly Older Guy who can be found wandering around malls at three o'clock in the afternoon with a glazed look in his eyes. But have an explanation ready in case someone questions you ("I decided to spend some time finding myself").

Come up with something useful to do. Obviously, you can't spend the next couple of decades cleaning out the attic. And there are just so many theories on the Natural Order of Things you can get out of fly-fishing.

Try to stick to your field. If you've spent a lifetime in vinyl flooring, keep at it, using your home as a base. On the other hand, if you've had it with your old occupation ("What's refrigeration ever done for me?"), it might be time to strike out in a fresh new direction.

Here are some possibilities:

CORPORATE DOWNSIZING CONSULTANT

Basically, this means throwing people out of work. You can start with the individual who downsized you and downsize him back.

LOUNGE SINGER

Agreeable work if your voice is pleasant and you were forced as a child to take piano lessons. Most of the good ones go down to Palm Beach in the winter, so there's a chance to fill in at restaurants in the Hamptons, for example, during the bitter cold months when there's no one there. Dress neatly, smile a lot to cover up mistakes, and play softly so that you don't drown out dinner-table conversation. Learn the standards and don't interpret anything. "Fly Me to the Moon" doesn't need your interpretation. Always credit the composer of the song so that the audience doesn't think you wrote it. Refer to at least one of the songwriters as "my good friend," as in "my good friend Billy Joel." Make pained faces during love songs to show that you've experienced what's in the song and that it's tearing you up personally. And learn the customers' favorites. The Rose family will beam with pride and come back again and again if the second they walk in you start playing "Everything's Coming Up Roses."

SCREENPLAY WRITING

Everyone is doing it. You don't dare show your face at parties unless you're working on a first draft. President Clinton

is reported to have a screenplay over at TriStar with a good shot at getting it made if they can interest De Niro.

Start by taking a course. Most of the people who teach them have never had a movie made—so you can learn from their mistakes.

LIMO DRIVER

Easy to crack into and can be lucrative. Your maturity, as a Slightly Older Guy, is a guarantee to the passenger that he's not going to be involved in a disabling accident. Dress neatly and keep the limo clean. It can really diminish the experience for the passenger if he finds candy wrappers in the backseat. Keep your foot steady, your eyes on the road, and let the passenger do the talking; he didn't spend all that money so he could hear about your knee operation.

Go out of your way to be nice to widows. It's a long shot, but they've been known to leave their fortunes to courteous limo drivers.

TEACHER

Many Slightly Older Guys are afraid of this field because they think it means teaching courses in the seventeenth-century French novel. That isn't the case at all. The jobs that make sense for the Slightly Older Guy are in community colleges—where you can draw on your experience. If it's in seamless gutters, you'll get to pass on everything you know about the profession, even if you were thrown out of it. The most important thing in teaching is to assure the other teachers that you're not out to get their jobs. And that you don't want tenure. That will help them relax so you can concentrate on your work, most of which is telling the students to shut up so you can talk.

Still, it's a noble profession, and there's always the possibility that one of your students will rise to the top and offer you a job.

MAÎTRE D'

Here again, your appearance, as a Slightly Older Guy, is assurance to the customer that he's going to be treated courteously and that the food is edible. Tell customers how glad you are to see them, and don't ask them why they insist on eating in other restaurants. Suggest that they have a seat at the bar and you'll see what you can do about a table—even if the place is half empty. When a customer places an order for the special, compliment him on his choice—but you don't have to tell him how fresh it is. It's supposed to be fresh. Don't get insulted if the customer gives you a small tip. Forty cents is forty cents.

And remember that your name isn't John anymore. It's Gianni.

ACTING

It's never too late to start. If they're shooting a movie in your town, try to get signed on as an extra. If you're hired and asked to be in a crowd scene, just blend into the background. Be yourself. Don't try to come off as the new James Dean. As a Slightly Older Guy, you're better off coming across as the new Ed Asner.

During the production, make friends with the director and tell him how much you liked that picture he did that bombed at the box office. See if he'll give you a speaking part, even one line, which will kick you into another financial bracket. When you open your mouth to say the line and nothing comes out, don't be discouraged. They'll be happy to do another sixteen takes—to justify the huge budget.

You can only move ahead as an actor if the camera likes you. Unfortunately, there's nothing much you can do about this. It's not as if you can take the camera out for a drink. It either likes you or it doesn't.

If you're asked to do a second picture, you'll have to join the Screen Actors Guild, which has wonderful insurance coverage for nervous breakdowns.

MEMOIRIST

You may have been thrown out of a job, but that doesn't mean you haven't led a fascinating life. It might even be fascinating enough for a memoir. Publishers are sick and tired of dirt on the Kennedys and might just feel it's time for *your* story—the ups and downs of a Slightly Older Guy. But it does have to be colorful.

It helps if you were abused as a child. Never mind that you were treated with unrelenting kindness. That still constitutes abuse.

It's useful, too, if you were in Nam, organizing Montagnards. Anything with Montagnards is good. And if you've slept with a few film stars, you're in an excellent position. But you have to have actually slept with them. Taking Ann-Margret out for a pizza doesn't count.

If your most memorable experience was the time you got Liza Minnelli's autograph at a gas station, you might want to hold off writing your memoirs until your life fills out a bit more.

The Last Word:
Wills, Burial Plots, Epitaphs

Wills are important. You won't find anyone who will argue against wills. But you may have put off making one out because there appears to be plenty of time for such things. Or because you're afraid of stirring up the gods.

"Why look for trouble?" you might ask. "And what's the rush? I'm feeling fine. It's not as if I'm putting up a courageous battle against some slow-wasting disease. I have a whole lifetime ahead of me to deal with such things."

It's a harsh thought, but let's be realistic—as a Slightly Older Guy, you no longer *have* a whole lifetime ahead of you. And there's no guarantee that you'll get to put up a struggle against a slow-wasting disease. Some of them aren't all that slow-wasting. And what if you're hit by a brick? Or fall victim to a drug-related drive-by shooting?

"Still and all," you might insist, "the very thought of writing a will makes me uneasy. It's as if I've agreed to pack it in.

"No more *New York Times* in the morning," you might go on dramatically. "No more *Court TV*. Never again to see the tides come in at Amagansett or to visit my nephew in Oregon.

"No more Connie Chung."

Such thoughts are unnecessarily macabre. The above scenario might play out at some point, but not *because* you've made out a will. To the best of available knowledge, people who have them live every bit as long as those who don't, and possibly a few weeks longer, since they won't have to walk

around with the nagging feeling that they should have made
out a will.

Once you're committed to doing it, make sure to proceed
in the proper manner. A will scribbled on an old cocktail
napkin might amuse a probate judge, but is unlikely to go
unchallenged. The key here is a lawyer, and since the fees
can be high, be sure to take some time to formulate your
thoughts. You don't want to change your mind every five
minutes while the meter's running. Believe it or not, there
are Slightly Older Guys who've left their families penniless
because they spent every dime on writing and rewriting their
wills.

Being of Sound Mind and Body

A decent provision should be made for loved ones, of
course. A wife will generally go to the top of the list, assuming she's of good character and won't hand over your
life's savings to the first moneygrubbing turkey who comes
sniffing around just days after the funeral.

Feelings about children should be kept in balance. You
don't, in a fit of pique, want to cut off a favored son because
you're still paying off his phone-sex charges. Recall his days
as a youngster and the fun you had dragging him off to Scout
meetings. Provide for him accordingly.

Surviving relatives generally prefer cash, as opposed, for
example, to old volleyball trophies or signed photographs
of Mayor Koch.

In general, you'll want your will to reflect your essential
decency and not veer off in a spiteful direction. If you've
always loathed a particular individual, there's no need to
point a finger at him in a special codicil: "Not a nickel for
Ed Greenspan. What did the sonofabitch ever do for me?"
Simply eliminate all mention of Greenspan.

If you're short on loved ones, consider setting up a foun-
dation as a means of perpetuating yourself in a favorable

light—and sidestepping onerous taxes. Medical foundations are a favorite for the high-minded. This option, of course, makes sense only for the well-heeled. There's no point in setting up a trust fund so that twelve dollars a month can be doled out for studying the kidney.

Time to Pack It In

Very much in vogue these days is the Living Will, which is designed to instruct relatives and physicians as to the conditions under which you'd prefer to be removed from the playing field. It's unlikely you'll want to be maintained in a vegetative state. But who knows? A Slightly Older Guy who's led a difficult life might find it pleasant to linger on for a few more years enjoying the bland and untroubled existence of an eggplant.

Most will agree there's no point in staying in the game when the brain is no longer directing the offense. But this is a tricky area and you'll no doubt want to make your own decision should this ever come about.

A sample Living Will might stipulate the following:

Please pull the plug if I should:

- Show an interest in soccer.
- Ask to have *The Bridges of Madison County* read aloud to me.
- Develop a craving for tofu.
- Begin anecdotes with the phrase "Funnily enough."

Here Lies . . .

Once you've signed off on a will, you'll want to deposit a copy with your lawyer—but it's also wise to keep one around the house in case your lawyer himself drops out of the frame. Be sure that it's relatively easy to find. There's no need to keep it posted on the front door where appliance salesmen can get a look at it—but you don't want to be too clever and hide it away, for example, in a hollowed-out copy of *Martin Chuzzlewit* where nobody can find it.

To further put your mind at ease, consider making some arrangement for your burial, so that surviving relatives won't have to flail about wondering how to proceed once you're gone. For the convenience of all parties, choose a stone in advance. And don't think along the lines of Grant's Tomb. Keep it modest in size, and make an effort to pay it off in advance. To have a gravestone bill rolling in each month can be unsettling to your survivors. As to the actual site of your stone, keep your demands simple and don't insist, for example, that you be laid to rest alongside Freud or Janis Joplin.

A fitting epitaph is in order. Many will choose to keep it upbeat and lighthearted:

- "All in all it's been a highly decent experience."
- "I wouldn't have missed it for the world."
- "So much for all that jogging."

Others will want to set forth the achievement that best exemplifies their life.

- "In '87, he took U.S. Sneakers to a record sales high."
- "He was one of the writers on *Tootsie*."

Only the insensitive will disregard the feelings of graveside visitors and couch their epitaphs in anguished terms: "For God's sake, get me out of here."

If cremation is your choice, don't burden your survivors with exotic demands—such as insisting that your ashes be scattered about at an Italian street festival or flung in the face of the president of MasterCard. Keep it simple. And for the Slightly Older Guy who asks that he be cryogenically frozen—to be slapped awake at some future date—remember that the best of canisters may eventually leak. Its usually the preference of a Slightly Older Guy to just fade away, not melt.

Once you've made the necessary arrangements, you may experience a feeling of serenity, knowing that if you suddenly bite the dust, your affairs will be in order. Remember, however, there's no need to hurry the process along so that everyone can see how magnanimous you've been. All concerned parties will be enriched in due time.

Part Five

The Large
Arena

A Run for Office

With legislators complaining that they're not allowed
to steal anymore—and being drummed out of politics at a
record clip—it might be time to consider a try for public
office. As a Slightly Older Guy, there's no question that
you're seasoned enough. And at the same time, you can
present yourself as a "fresh face," someone who feels we're
headed down the "wrong" road and wants to steer us in the
"right" direction. There's no point in trying to unseat Newt
Gingrich on your first go-round. Start at the local level and
see if there's a political group that will have you. Ones called
the Integrity Party generally do well. If there's something
shady in your background, get the word out in advance, so
that you're not unmasked in mid-campaign as a pedophile
or a tax cheat or lord-knows-what.

Lose some weight, do something about your hair, and
develop an agenda. Following are some suggestions along
that line.

WHAT YOU'RE IN FAVOR OF

- Getting America back on its feet.
- Getting government off our backs. (How else can we
  get on our feet?)
- The ordinary American (provided he's not too
  ordinary).

261

- A strong dollar. But not too strong. We don't need an Arnold Schwarzenegger of a dollar, one that frightens off our trading partners. Just one that's strong enough so that they don't kick sand in our face.
- Some action on interest rates. Raise them, lower them, just do *something* with them.
- More cops on the beat. And they have to live in the community they're patrolling, not in Beverly Hills.
- Getting rid of the fat in government, including the overfed incumbent.
- A working relationship with the Russians so long as he doesn't (a) ask for money and (b) start acting like a Russian.
- Building more prisons—in some other community.
- A strong defense, as long as it doesn't require throwing all of our money into weapons.
- Bringing the Japanese into line. If necessary, you'll send someone over there to scold them again.

WHAT YOU'RE OPPOSED TO

- Pie-in-the-sky solutions to our problems.
- Big government. Then again, you don't want a government that's too small, either. What you'd like to see is one that's just the right size.
- Those who stand against us.
- Coddling criminals. Coddling the Japanese, the French, coddling anyone, for that matter. You just don't approve of coddling.
- Wars that are not in our national interest. But once we decide what our national interest is, you might be in favor of one or two little ones now and then.
- Violence on TV. Obviously, your opponent can't get enough of it.
- The media. You'd like to see the press live up to its responsibilities and stop attacking you.

ONCE THE CAMPAIGN IS UNDER WAY

- Explain that you're not going to answer your opponent's charges. To do so would only dignify them. And the last thing you need is to have dignified charges thrown at you.
- Complain that your opponent is trying to buy the election, which is unfair, since you can't afford to do the same.
- Accuse him of knuckling under to special interests. And you know for a fact they're not that special.
- Hire a pollster to show you're closing the gap— and should peak on Election Day.

SHOULD YOU WIN

- Congratulate your opponent on a hard-fought campaign, and tell him you agree with a surprising number of his proposals. Ask if he'd mind if you adopted them as your own.
- Tell your supporters that your work has just begun—even though you know it's over.
- Don't renege on your campaign promises until at least a few months have gone by.

SHOULD YOU LOSE

- Congratulate your opponent and say that you didn't mean most of the terrible things you said about him. Tell him it was the heat of the campaign that made you call him a dickhead.
- At a press conference, say that the only reason you lost is that your message didn't get out.
- Issue a statement saying that anyone who subjects himself and his family to the abuse of a political campaign has got to be insane—and then start planning your next one.

A Word about P.C.

Of all Americans, it's the Slightly Older Guy who can remember vividly what seemed to be sunnier times—when it was possible fearlessly to scramble up a dozen eggs, puff a cigar in public, have a friend named Shorty, and not worry about tipping your hat to a woman for fear of being thought condescending.

No wonder, then, that you may have found yourself experiencing a vague feeling of unease, a sense that no matter what you do or say, you're going to be called a dinosaur or an unfeeling clod. Nothing has prepared you for an America that's told you to Get Sensitive or Get Out.

There are several ways to deal with this glum phenomenon:

- You can, of course, continue defiantly to wolf down bacon cheeseburgers, blow smoke in every direction, and stubbornly continue to use words like "mankind" and "stewardess."
- Or you can shut yourself off from most of the world, restrict your circle to a few trusted friends, and only frequent bars in which it's permitted to say "broads" and "fatso."
- And then there's a third option, which may turn out to be the most intelligent, and is certainly the least taxing. Step back a bit. Concede that, on balance, P.C. isn't all that bad, that Shorty never really did

enjoy the name, that a female acquaintance, possibly heading up Barnard now, was not happy about being thought of as someone with "a great set of lungs."

It's not inconsistent to follow that third course in principle but still refuse to say "waitperson."

Part Six

Ease On Down the Road

Making Your Life Comfortable

As a Slightly Older Guy, you have a right to be every bit as comfortable as your fellow Americans. Here are some thoughts on how to make your days a bit more pleasant than they might otherwise be.

DO ONE THING AT A TIME

There are some people who can crack a code while they're varnishing an end table, but they're few in number and they're not happy.

LISTEN

It may be that you were born in India and orphaned at five and that yours is a fascinating story. But other people have intriguing stories as well. Try listening to one. If it starts to drag, you can always cut in and resume telling yours.

GET UP EARLY

If you rise at six, for example, you'll find that you have a whole day extra to play with. But don't go back to bed at noon or you'll spoil the effect.

BLOW ON YOUR SOUP BEFORE TAKING
THE FIRST SPOONFUL

This is especially true in the case of onion soup au gratin, with that large smoldering lid on it.

ALWAYS CARRY INSURANCE

Statistically speaking, it's not a good bet, but do it anyway. It will make you feel better. One advantage of taking out insurance, generally, is that you get to hate the insurance industry.

ELIMINATE GUILT

If you're responsible for the collapse of a company or the death of a pet, guilt feelings are not going to restore the company to financial health or bring back your canary. So get rid of them. They're only useful as a sexual stimulant.

LIE STILL IF YOU SLIP ON THE ICE

There's no need to leap to your feet in a demonstration of fitness. Just stay there for a while and clear your head—unless someone tremendously attractive is watching.

DON'T FIGHT FOR SLEEP

There's nothing that says that as an American you're entitled to eight hours of it, that it's owed to you, like Social Security. If you can't get to sleep, have a glass of warm milk and read Solzhenitsyn. In no time at all, you'll feel drowsy. And you'll have gotten some Solzhenitsyn out of the way.

TIGHTEN UP ON YOUR READING OF
THE OBITUARIES

It's all right to glance at a few, but you don't have to send out for newspapers in distant cities for ones you may have missed. When you skip the sports page and go straight to the obits, take it as a warning.

DON'T MAKE RESERVATIONS TOO FAR
IN ADVANCE

What if, six months from now, you've lost interest in the Siberian Reindeer Dance Troupe? Aren't you better off waiting until the last minute and hoping someone will cancel— someone who never wanted to see the Siberians in the first place?

DON'T DANCE UNLESS YOU FEEL LIKE DANCING

ENJOY THE MOMENT

Does it have to be pointed out that there aren't quite as many left to enjoy? If you have tickets to a Knicks game, don't pace up and down until the big day. It's permissible to have fun while you're waiting.

Back on the Highway

Much has been made of the American and his romance with the automobile—and for good reason. He may be a minor player at home or at the office, but on the open road he's a star.

Of no one is this more true than the Slightly Older Guy. So maybe he's lost a step—but his car hasn't. Behind the wheel of a proud Pontiac Marquis or a humble Subaru, you might drive alongside a college president, share the highway with leading members of the Clinton administration, or receive the same traffic ticket as Microsoft's William Gates.

As you breeze along the road, there's no need for you to feed the dog or take out the garbage. On the highway, state tax collectors can't get their hands on you.

In short, you're free to be the Slightly Older Guy at his liberated, uninhibited best.

Your Car as a Statement

It's difficult, of course, to be at your best in a broken-down gas-eater. If you can manage it, try to build up your confidence with the purchase of a new car.

"What good will that do?" you might ask. "Even in a new Plymouth Duster, I'll still be a little down in the mouth."

That's not necessarily true. You may be down in the mouth precisely because you're not in a new Plymouth Duster.

Deciding which car to drive is of tremendous importance since—whether you like it or not—your selection is going to become the most important part of your identity. Never mind that you've written a sonnet for the last Inauguration, or ironed out kinks in the Genome Project—around town you'll still be known as "the guy in the green Volvo." So pick a car that you want to represent you. If it turns out to be a Dodge Shadow, so be it. As long as you can look at the car and say, "That Dodge Shadow is me."

Loyalty

Brand loyalty, of course, will be a factor in your selection. It may be that you've been a Cougar man for some time and have no intention of changing. You might even want that for your epitaph: "Here lies Paul Feinschreiber. He stayed with Cougars, right to the end."

That's all very admirable, but it's also true that switching over to another brand—becoming a Buick Skylark fellow, for example—can be a heady and rewarding experience. And don't worry about the Cougar people. They'll hardly miss you.

Standing Up to the Salesman

Once you've zeroed in on a favorite model, don't be afraid to question the price. There's a good deal of give here, and it's not as if the salesman is going to report you as a haggler to your friends.

Be sure, in your negotiations, to throw out a few technical phrases so that you don't come off as an easy mark. Ask the salesman about torque. That's bound to put him on the defensive, since nobody really knows what it is, other than that it's a good thing and you want to have some of it working in your favor.

Once you have the salesman on the defensive, inspect the car carefully, but don't kick the tires. Many younger salesmen don't understand the custom and will kick you back.

Stroke your chin thoughtfully as you look beneath the hood. Take a good look. If you're an average driver, it's probably the last time you'll look under there. And don't be confused by what you see. The only ones who understand the engine are a few aging rocket scientists from Nazi Germany.

Testing a Car—What to Look For

VISIBILITY

Make sure the visibility is such that you can see other drivers sneaking up on you.

THE "FEEL" OF THE ROAD

Terribly important for certain drivers. For some odd reason, they're not happy unless they can feel the road beneath them. For others, if they've felt it once, that's plenty.

ANTILOCK BRAKES

Take all claims about brakes with a grain of salt. If it's really slippery, there's no way to stop a car other than to drag your foot on the ground.

THE SMELL

Don't be seduced by the smell of a new car. They all smell nice for a few days, and you don't want to pay $30,000 for a car because it smells nice. Besides, you can purchase "new car smell in a can" for about $3.95 at most drugstores.

Your Fellow Drivers

Driving defensively is always a good idea. Be wary of cars that are less expensive than yours, since their drivers may be out to get you. Contrarily, if the owner of a luxury car passes you with a sneer, pay no attention to him. If you absolutely have to, sneer back.

From time to time, you'll encounter a fellow who's driving the same model as you. If he waves at you, there's no need to stop, introduce yourself, and invite him to dinner. A simple return wave will suffice.

Troopers and Tito Puente

Beware of playing infectious music on your car radio, Latin songs in particular. It's difficult to control a car while you're doing a merengue.

If a trooper should happen to pull you over for speeding, it's unseemly to whine and insist on your innocence. Accept his decision stoically and say you're glad *someone* is doing his job well. He'll give you a summons anyway, but at least you'll send him off with a good feeling.

Return of the Germans

Although car-jacking has become a somber reality, it's fruitless to stay awake at night worrying about it. The Germans, for example, have taken serious losses in Miami, yet they've returned in force. (Admittedly, many are disguised as Frenchmen.) If someone insists on stealing your car at gunpoint, don't try to bargain by offering to take him for a spin. And by no means lecture him about the harsh conditions he'll face in prison. Simply hand him the keys and be flattered that he's chosen *your* car, not just anyone's.

A new car isn't going to change your life entirely. It isn't as if women on both sides of the street will keel over when you drive by in your new Honda. But at least you'll be a Slightly Older Guy with mobility.

And if things get hairy, your car will always be there in the driveway, a faithful friend, ready to whisk you out of town in a hurry.

Slightly Older Guy Treats

As a Slightly Older Guy, there are bound to be moments when you'll feel like just sitting around and quietly waiting for the final curtain. At such times, well-meaning friends will advise you to reach out beyond yourself and help others—by manning a suicide hotline or taking a homeless person to lunch at Le Cirque. These are well-meaning gestures, but they're a bit on the flashy side, and you don't want to neglect yourself entirely. There are treats to be had that are not only affordable, but won't make you feel you've let down the disadvantaged.

Here are some suggestions:

Theatre

Along with the rest of the world, you're no doubt "into film" and have probably forgotten that the theatre, although gasping, still lives. It may be disorienting to watch an entertainment in which Bruce Willis isn't on hand to hold it all together for you—but once you've settled in and gotten used to it, it will be fun to watch live actors converse without hysteria and to have an occasional shard of intelligence fly out at you. A word of caution, however. There are many plays that are directed at "those of us who wish to support the theatre." Stay away from them, and also avoid plays in which the actors come down into the audience and tousle

your hair—or ones in which you're dragged up on stage and
asked to fill in as part of a jeering mob.

Spectator Sports

Spectator sports are an excellent leisure activity for the
Slightly Older Guy who still wants to compete but has to
face the fact that he's become a slow healer.

THE NFL

It's billed as a game of strategy, but basically, professional
football is about *hitting*—which you, the Slightly Older Guy,
in the comfort and safety of your living room, won't be called
on to do. Players are getting bigger by the minute: a 275-
pound offensive tackle is now considered puny and is taking
his life in his hands when he steps on the field. Blocking, tackling, and passing, once staples of the game, are no longer considered half as important as creative dancing in the end zone.

THE NBA

There's no need to watch a basketball game in its entirety
since the owners, in a secret covenant, have agreed that the
outcome of all games is to be decided in the final five minutes. Once you're aware of this, you can go out for a leisurely
dinner and then nip back to catch the last few points, which
are the only ones of any importance.

Jamal Mashburn, Muggsy Bogues, Anfernee Hardaway,
Alonzo Mourning, Sedale Threatt. No contest here! NBA
players have the best names of any sport.

BOXING

Having been given the imprimatur of Joyce Carol Oates,
boxing no longer has to be enjoyed in stealth. And long-in-

the-tooth fighters such as George Foreman, Larry Holmes, and Roberto Duran have done wonders to put the Slightly Older Guy on the map.

The major change that's come about in the sport is the bewildering number of titles and weight classes. There are at least forty thin little fellows going around insisting they're superbantamweight champions. To qualify for a championship belt, a fighter needs only to have beaten up more people than anyone else in his neighborhood.

BASEBALL

Each game takes a lifetime. Bearable if thought of as a metaphor for something larger—the slow passage of time, for example. For some real action, catch the contract negotiations.

Keep Your Perspective

One of the dangers of spectator sports is overclose identification with your team. As an example:

FADE IN . . .

Sunday afternoon, and HARRY, a Slightly Older Guy, stands dejectedly in the front hall of his house, his bags packed. His wife GRETA approaches.

HARRY: I'm leaving.
GRETA: The Giants?
HARRY: What else?
GRETA: Maybe they'll win next week.
HARRY: (*bitterly*)
Maybe I'll win the lottery.
(*Lifts bags*)

GRETA: But where will you go? What will you do?
HARRY: Frankly, Greta, I don't give a damn.
He turns, opens door, leaves.

FADE OUT . . .

Don't let this happen to you A sure sign of overclose identification with your team is when you start to say "*We* lost
again" or "*We* sure looked good out there." Remember that
it was the *Giants* who lost, not you. And that when your
favorite quarterback is intercepted half a dozen times in a
championship game, it's unfortunate, but *he* did the screw-
ing up. *You're* not the one who has to hide your head in
shame, endure taunts from outraged fans, and be upset until
you redeem yourself next season. *He* is.
For God's sake, remember that.

In Praise of Prose

When it's recommended that he return to the pleasure of
reading, the Slightly Older Guy, whose shelves are overflow-
ing with books, is likely to say: "I'd love to, but I can't find
anything to read. And don't tell me about light fiction. It's
too light."

The observation may have some truth to it, but there's
never been a law saying you can't go back to books you've
enjoyed as a Slightly Younger Guy. *Mr. Midshipman Easy*
may be pushing the envelope a bit, but a return trip to *The
Great Gatsby* or *The Catcher in the Rye* or Waugh's *A Handful of Dust* will find any of them holding up staunchly. Re-
visiting *The Plague* may set you back a bit, but with your
accumulated wisdom you may find yourself finally break-
ing through on *Ulysses.*

To be on the safe side, stay away from *The Old Man and
the Sea.*

Get Out of Town

There's something *final* about foreign travel, and the Slightly Older Guy may have been avoiding it for fear of never being able to make it back home. But you don't have to think of it that way. If you've enjoyed Smolensk, there's no reason why you can't plan a return to Smolensk year after year until you're sick of it.

Here are some other possibilities:

EASTERN EUROPE

Prague, Budapest, Gdansk. There's not much going on other than churches and a tremendous amount of shopping, most of it for discontinued jogging suits.

THE MIDDLE EAST

Too dangerous, obviously, unless you dress up as a Druse. And even as a Druse, you can get caught in the line of fire. Wait for a few more peace treaties.

THE FAR EAST

A whole different story, and Tokyo, in particular, is not to be missed. It's a city with surprises waiting for you at every turn. Tiny little tilted skyscrapers, crows in your hotel room, grandmothers happily shining your shoes, then jumping on your back to give you a massage. The world's best *Chinese* food, of all things. Discourtesies, of course, followed by tremendous acts of kindness, such as a waiter in the dead of night crossing the entire city to return your credit card. Streets so safe that you may find yourself longing for a little violence. And a field day for the lonely. Japan is the loneliest country in the world; it's just out there, all by itself, not quite Eastern, not quite Western, not sure exactly what it is. At lunchtime, a million heavily madeup secretaries sit in fast-food restaurants and stare out at the streets, wondering if they'll ever find a soul mate, which of course they won't because of all the makeup. The reason that the Japanese strike out at other countries now and then is not for raw materials, but so they can get around and try to make new friends. Many people don't understand that.

CANADA

Another lonely country, but at least it's just sitting there in all its indolence and not hurting anyone.

THE U.S.A.

"Don't tell me about America," you might say when someone suggests domestic travel. "I've already seen it."

That may be true, but have you seen it lately? Pittsburgh, for example, has come a long way since the last time you were there, and now has trees. There are glorious national parks, such as Arcadia National in Maine, that only three or four people know about and are not that boring.

And don't overlook New Jersey, which is a fascinating state and much closer to New York than you might realize.

So there you are, a sampling of diversions, and only a partial one. The range is dizzying—leathercraft, Gaelic dancing, membership in a cult—and all there for the Slightly Older Guy who refuses to give up the ghost.

The Country Life

If you're a Slightly Older Guy who's grown weary of the bright lights, you might want to consider a move to the countryside. It's not a matter of "putting yourself out to pasture." No one is saying that. You're simply choosing a quieter life.

There's no need to bury yourself in Montana with environmentalists. What you want is a town that's close enough to the city so that you can make a run for it if the healthful country life becomes oppressive. On the other hand, you don't want to be *too* close or you'll find yourself popping in at every opportunity and spending more time in the city than you did when you lived there. Ideal is a vacation community where you can enjoy a quiet eight or nine months until Calvin Klein arrives in the summer to liven things up.

"But I've lived all my *life* in the city," you might say. "There's no Stuttgart Ballet out in the sticks. They probably don't have any Thai restaurants either. What if I get a toothache? Who do I see about it, a blacksmith?

"And more to the point, what would I do out there?"

The New Countryside

To begin with, you don't have to *do* much of anything. That's the whole point. You probably *did* too much in the city. Isn't that what turned you into a prematurely Slightly Older Guy? Then, too, stop thinking of the country as being made up of sleepy little backwoods hamlets. Many villages are hooked up to cable so that you don't have to miss a single segment of *Empty Nest*. Professional people have flocked to the countryside, many of them psychiatrists who can explain to you why you needed to get out of the city. And you don't have to be cut off from the world. Computer technology is such that you can be in constant touch with Bangladesh.

It's true that the cultural level sags a bit as you move away from the city, but it's rare that you won't be able to track down at least one church group that's doing *Antigone*. And sumptuous meals are available for $5.95 at places like Ralph's Diner, which becomes Chez Ralph's during the summer and charges weekenders $59.95 for the same menu.

Don't get the feeling that you're going to be neglected. The locals will be happy to keep you company once you've convinced them that you're not out there to throw up condominiums. Fellow Slightly Older Guys generally congregate at the post office in the morning, many of them limping conspicuously, others carting away their mail with surprising vigor. In short order, you'll be invited along to join them at the local coffee shop for landfill discussions.

Woodstoves, geese, plenty of elbow room—all in all, not a bad little life for the Slightly Older Guy who's ready to scale back his operation.

If you decide to make the move, you can also expect the following:

A ROUGH FIRST NIGHT

No sirens. No bus exhaust. No bloodcurdling arguments in the next apartment. Nothing but unrelenting silence, and a temptation on your part to chuck it all and go back to the city, where you can at least count on a few gunshots to shake things up. If this happens, relax. Have a glass of warm milk. Tell yourself: "I'm going to make it. The peace and quiet is not going to kill me."

A SLOWER PACE

It's not atypical for a city-dwelling Slightly Older Guy to make a nuisance of himself when he first arrives in the country—barging into the general store, demanding that the clerk drop everything and show him the latest in farm implements. It's a style, of course, that's not going to win you any friends. Not to fear—in time, you'll find yourself falling in with the slower country rhythm. Before long, you'll think nothing of spending an entire morning deciding on a paint thinner.

A SURPRISING LACK OF PRIVACY

Seems odd, with all that space. Yet everyone knows everyone else in a small town, and you can expect your every move to be recorded. This closeness of community can be comforting if you're a flood victim, but not if you're thinking of an affair, which may have to be carried out in a duck blind.

DIFFERENT CONCERNS

Expect a great deal of talk about the weather. About this year's winter. And how it was nothing compared to the one in '78. Be patient. You can't expect people in small towns to be up on Jeffrey Katzenberg's career moves. Give them some room. And when someone comments on the heavy rainfall, be sure to say, "I guess we really needed it."

NO FULL ACCEPTANCE

There's always a family named Bagley or Crenshaw who founded the town and has been there for hundreds of years. Don't expect them to welcome you with open arms, or to become part of their crowd. It's possible to marry your way in, but since you're a Slightly Older Guy it's probably a little late for that. Bide your time. Don't look too anxious. Eventually, you'll be invited to one of their charity benefits—for a sizable donation.

NATURAL DISASTERS

They're part of the package. Stock up on candles and powdered milk. Study the evacuation routes. If you're in a coastal area, expect to be featured on the news every now and then as a twister victim who's had half his house shorn away. (And hope that Al Gore gets out there in a hurry to assess the damage.)

Time passes slowly in the country, which is deceptive. It's possible to wake up one morning and find that you're eighty, which you may not want to be just yet.

And don't expect the city to have remained frozen in time during your absence. They've had to push on without you. When you go back for a visit, don't be shocked if there's a stranger sitting in a restaurant booth that had always been reserved for you. Expect old friends to look at you in puzzlement and wonder why you've suddenly got all that gray hair.

But at least you'll have survived. You won't have allowed the city to "eat you up." And if life in the country doesn't work out, on top of which your old apartment is taken, maybe you can find a suitable one down the hall.

Part Seven

The Future—
Such as It Is

Get Ready to Meet
Your Maker

As a Slightly Older Guy, it's no doubt dawned on you that you're not going to be in the game forever. You may have even caught a glimpse of the finish line, and in an anxious moment considered flinging yourself into the arms of a higher power. If it's been some time since you've been devotional, there are certain insecurities that are bound to arise.

"What if they won't take me back?" you might ask. "I haven't been to church in years. And suppose they get wind of my escapades in the Seventies? That one night alone in Frankfurt is enough to disqualify me right there. Is a kinky guy allowed to return to the fold?"

As it happens, the news is good in this area. The faiths have always been forgiving. Now—battered by charges of mischief in the churchyard, taken to task for exclusionary positions on gays, women, abortion—they're inclined to be more welcoming than ever.

In a sense, you'll be taking each other back.

"But you don't understand the extent of it," you might persist. "I've never taken any of this seriously. For some time, I went around saying that God was a waiter."

Here again, there's no cause for concern. No matter what the extent of your blasphemy, the chances are strong you'll he happily piped aboard. And it isn't as if a ledger is being kept on your transgressions—or that you'll be penalized for the lateness of your conversion. There's no need to play catch-up here.

Hold the Curtain!

Once you've put yourself in a prayerful stance, you can happily contemplate an afterlife in which you're lolling about on a cloud—or perhaps amusingly reincarnated as a four-legged creature. Those residing on the West Coast will no doubt see themselves returning as part of the universal order, blending seamlessly into the cosmos.

There is, however, the Slightly Older Guy who'll have none of this and takes a baleful view of the whole business. "I'm not interested in returning as a gazelle," he'll say. "And don't talk to me about being hooked to the tail of some bloody comet. That's not going to do me any good if I want to watch CNN. I'm having a fine time of it just the way things are.

"Why does it all have to end?"

There's no dealing with such a fellow except to remind him that he hasn't exactly spent his life watching a flop show. It isn't as if he's been strapped to a chair for decades watching *Ishtar*. As a Slightly Older Guy of a certain age, he's been present at a cavalcade of events unparalleled in human history. He's seen Fascist Germany brought to its knees, space invaded, the earth computerized, the genetic code laid bare, mighty communism fallen apart like a wet Kleenex. Surely he can't complain about the cast of characters—feisty Truman, inscrutable Mao, dogged Castro, the amazing actor slash president Ronald Reagan, loopy Bush, Tom Snyder, and towering above them all for sheer entertainment value, the nefariously great Richard Nixon.

When the curtain comes down on this astonishing show, is it too much to ask that he give up his seat to another theatregoer?

"That's all very well," you might say, "but if I could only have one more shot at being a young guy."

Is that what you really want?

As the years have spun along, you may have come to think of your early days as an idyllic romp, an unending series of blissful escapades. But let's face it. You were lucky you didn't end up on Rikers Island.

Youth, of course, continues to have its frisky appeal. But isn't it possible that it's the Slightly Older Guy, his passions in balance, his judgment seasoned by time (and a bit of bounce left in his legs), who's best positioned to enjoy the very cream of existence?

Such a case can he put forward by the Slightly Older Guy with the energy to make it and the capacity to believe such things.

In Sum

Tick, Tick, Tick

As a Slightly Older Guy, it's time to get your act together.

"But I don't *have* an act," you might say. "That's always been the problem."

Then get one. And you can start by tying up loose ends. If you have an estranged child out there, call and patch things up. Vote for once in your life. And if you've loved someone for thirty years, let that person in on it before she goes into a nursing home.

Take some positions. If you've been waffling for years on multilateral export controls, come down on one side or the other. Decide once and for all what your feelings are about Jack Kemp.

"But nobody *cares* what I think," you might say in protest. "There are much smarter guys out there."

That's not quite true. Maybe there *were* smarter guys, but they may not be out there anymore. That's the whole point. As a Slightly Older Guy, you'll be revered for your wisdom, not that anyone is necessarily interested in what you have to say but because there are so few alternatives.

Decide what you want out of life—or what's left of it—and go after it. No more sitting on the bench or warming up on the sidelines. You *have* to play because there's no one else on the field. What's the worst thing that can happen?

"The poor sonofabitch," someone will say. "He knew what he wanted and went after it."

Is that so bad?

Start now. Don't wait for a nice weekend. You're only a Slightly Older Guy once.

Seek peace. Who could possibly be down on peace? But don't seek too much or you'll end up resting in it while the parade passes by.

Play hard. Drink the wine. Never let it be said that you sat down at the banquet of life and settled for a few hors d'oeuvres.

Trot off into the sunset with the assurance that your legacy will be an enduring one.

The world is waiting to see how you deal with the third act of your personal drama. It's not going to be any walk in the park. Did anyone say it would be? But someone has to be a Slightly Older Guy, and it might as well be you. Be grateful that you were still around to take on the job.

The very best to you, Slightly Older Guy, as you get into your uniform and stumble bravely down the field toward an uncertain goal line. You may not see or hear it, but there's a cheering section out there, made up of others who will be following in your footsteps—a lot sooner than they realize. The least you can do is set a reasonable example for them. Rage, rage, rage against the night if you absolutely must— and if you think it will do any good—but have the grace to do so in private. And no matter how you choose to proceed, for God's sake: no whining.

The End
(of the book, not the Slightly Older Guy)

Afterword

The Considerably Older Guy

You've been a Lonely Guy and a Slightly Older Guy. Let's assume for the moment that you are still on board. It's time now to stagger on a bit and enter the less than cheery world of the Considerably Older Guy. This is bleak territory indeed. Only the brave need apply. It may very well be the end of the line—and it's not Ronkonkoma.

With a measure of anxiety, you might ask: *"How do I know when I've become a Considerably Older Guy?"*

There are little telltale signs such as a suspicion, generally well-founded, that everything hurts. It takes the better part of a morning to get dressed. Suddenly, all you want to do is sit around and watch tapes of World War II aerial battles over Britain. The name "Wendell Willkie" keeps reverberating in your head. The Victoria's Secret catalogue gets a quick riffle instead of its usual careful scrutiny. The clincher is when you're told repeatedly after meals that there are particles of food stuck to your lip.

"And then?" you ask.

And then it's downhill all the way.

"I'm starting to panic."

Don't. It's a waste of energy of which you have little to spare. Old friends who might sympathize and come to your aid may very well have gone on to their just rewards. Loved ones tend to live on the other coast. Best to grit your teeth— or gums, as it were—and push ahead. Remaining in place is bad for the joints. Too much movement is bad for the joints as well. Everything is bad for the joints.

"Is there anything good about this stage of life?"

Not really. However, as absurd as it sounds, there are several features that can, with a stretch of the imagination (stretching, actually, *is* good for the joints), be put in the positive column.

For one thing, on a battlefield that's become increasingly thinned out—and with comrades falling all about you—it's remarkable that you are here at all.

"So it's great just to be in the game, is that it?"

You're not *in* the game. That's the whole point. You're damned lucky to be sitting on the sidelines. What you want to focus on is that you're here at all. While you're doddering about in St. Petersburg, or wherever it is you end up, you might, to amuse your fellow survivors, want to state that fact on a T-shirt: I'M STILL HERE.

On the other hand, it's bad form to visit the local cemetery, thumb your nose at the gravestones, and add the words: AND YOU'RE NOT.

"Being a Considerably Older Guy doesn't sound like it's any fun."

Fun? Happiness? These are words it's best to set aside, and not just for the time being. What you want are small pleasures, minipleasures, if you will. Here are a few—and do try to remember them:

Friends. The thrill of making new ones. (Thinking of them as "replacements" is unhelpful.) It's true that most of your new friends will be doctors, but there is no reason why a gastroenterologist can't be a barrel of laughs. Just try to cultivate at least one friend who is in worse shape than you are.

Adventure. Surprisingly, there is no shortage of it. There's no need for the Considerably Older Guy to shoot the rapids or swim with sharks. The big challenge is for him to get out of bed in the morning and not pull something . . . or to put on a pair of socks and make it back to a standing position. (And if you call 911, that's cheating.)

What can possibly be more dangerous than getting trapped in a sweater? Or how about opening a ketchup bottle, knowing full well that one vigorous twist too many and it's all over.

Suspense. The life of the Considerably Older Guy is filled with it. Will he make it to the supermarket and back? Will he make it anywhere? More ambitiously, will the Big Fella (see Slightly Older Guy, page 173) be able to rouse himself from a deep slumber and give a decent account of himself?

"I just wish I had some guidelines..."
There are some, but those who've made it this far generally can't remember what they are. Nevertheless . . .

- Say farewell to stomach crunches.
- Adopt a philosophy—any old philosophy—just so long as you have one. Try to improve on Mario Puzo's assessment of the whole business: "We get old and we die."
- Put in a little time on your last words. It's never too early to start. You never know when the clock is going to strike midnight. Don't be embarrassed about this. Most Famous Last Words went through many rewrites. (Those with minimal verbal skills can keep a copy handy of the lyrics to the Lieber/ Stoller song "Is That All There Is?")
- Reduce contact with those who assure you that there are new generations coming along to take your place.
- When plugging in floor-level electrical appliances, put a pillow under your knees.

- Keep your composure when you ask a broker to recommend a long-term investment and he laughs in your face.
- Make sure you need a hip replacement before you have one. Don't do it just to spice up your life.
- Use a computer only with the full understanding that if it crashes, you'll probably crash with it.

And that's about it. Stay warm, don't trip, and carry lots of ID. And under no circumstances try to pick up Giselle Bundchen. Suppose the Brazilian hottie says, "What took you so long?" Then what do you do?

Generally speaking, it's best not to try to do too much. Collecting the mail may not seem like much to others, but at this stage of the game it's a day's work.

Good luck to you, Considerably Older Guy. Give yourself a pat on the back (easy does it) for having made it this far. As to that last stretch of road, don't despair. Think of all the fun Strom Thurmond has had.

BJF
New York City, 2001

Acknowledgments

The author is grateful to Fred Hills, Burton Beals, Laureen Connelly Rowland, Candida Donadio, Patricia J. O'Dono-hue, and Barbara Hoffman for getting him through this— if not quite carrying him on their backs.